AN HOUR IN THE DARKNESS

An Hour in the Darkness

You can still fall in love when you're crazy can't you...?

Michael Bailey

Copyright © 2014 Michael Bailey

The moral right of the author has been asserted.

Apart from any fair dealing for the purposes of research or private study, or criticism or review, as permitted under the Copyright, Designs and Patents Act 1988, this publication may only be reproduced, stored or transmitted, in any form or by any means, with the prior permission in writing of the publishers, or in the case of reprographic reproduction in accordance with the terms of licences issued by the Copyright Licensing Agency. Enquiries concerning reproduction outside those terms should be sent to the publishers.

Matador
9 Priory Business Park
Kibworth Beauchamp
Leicestershire LE8 0RX, UK
Tel: (+44) 116 279 2299
Fax: (+44) 116 279 2277
Email: books@troubador.co.uk
Web: www.troubador.co.uk/matador

ISBN 978 1784620 059

British Library Cataloguing in Publication Data.
A catalogue record for this book is available from the British Library.

Typeset in Goudy Old Style by Troubador Publishing Ltd
Printed and bound in the UK by TJ International, Padstow, Cornwall

Matador is an imprint of Troubador Publishing Ltd

MIX
Paper from
responsible sources
FSC® C013056

For Heather,
without whose love
I would be completely shipwreck'd.

1

Listen, if you're going to read this, you'd better understand something right from the start: I always found it difficult talking to girls. I always thought it was more about the things you didn't say. You just about break your head open trying to think of something clever when all they want to hear is that you love them. I really don't understand it too well. It's like they're virtually tearing themselves up inside until you've said it. Listen, they don't care if you mean it or not as long as you keep saying it. Girls are real insecure about that kind of thing. I sure spend too much time worrying in case I haven't told girls I love them enough.

Anyway, this is about that time I hurt my head and my life slid away from me for a while. I went off on my own and tried to find myself or something. I don't know. Anyway, I met this girl called Ronnie and sort of fell in love with her. You know how it is? It was the real thing and everything. I was crazy, I admit it, but you can still fall in love when you're crazy, can't you?

I was born in Leicester. It's in the Midlands somewhere. There's a huge clock tower in the centre that shines like a column of chalk. It overlooks the market where I met Ronnie.

I admit I tried to make Ronnie swoon and fall in love with me the first time I saw her. I think she was a little frightened of me, at first. Listen, she was terrified, okay? I know her crap awful boss hated me. Boy, he sure was the serious, insensitive type, if you ask me. At the end of the day I suppose some guys just aren't too romantic, and everything. I sure hate those fellers who put work before love, don't you?

Listen, before we go any further, you'd better understand that I really don't attach too much importance to work, okay? I can walk out of any job without looking back and I usually break all the young girls' hearts when I go. One day I'm the funniest person you've ever met and the next I'm a rude, arrogant son-of-a-bitch. The guy who made you laugh yesterday has gone, okay, and he's never coming back. Believe me, I know. Listen, as soon as things start to go well for me I have to smash it all down. I have to get away as quickly as possible. I have to go find some new place where I can start it all over again. If you can't join them, beat them. I think I try too hard to make people laugh and fall in love with me. Boy, it sure is exhausting living your life like that.

The fountain near the Town Hall is beautiful though, don't you think? The water glitters in the air for a second before it smashes on the ground next to your feet. When the sky over Leicester turns dark it reflects on the surface of the water with a wintry gleam or something. I don't know. I get confused sometimes. I'm not sure that last part is correct. I used to sit near the fountain for hours with my sister, Jenny, when we were both kids. Jenny used to hold my hand real tight in case the water went in her eyes. That fountain used to scare her half to death, but Jenny loved it anyway.

One afternoon, my girlfriend Karen came round to my parents' house and because I didn't know what to do with her I took her into the back room to play darts. While she was taking her coat off I had to tell her about a million times that I loved her; she sure was the sensitive, lacking in self-confidence type. Karen told me it had taken her about a million years to make herself look pretty for me. Boy, I sure felt depressed when she told me that. Please don't spend so long making yourself pretty for me, okay? You put a hell of a lot of responsibility on someone when you tell them it took you about a million years to get ready.

Anyway, I told Karen I loved her some more to make up for it. Of course, I didn't love her; I just told her that to make myself feel better. Karen sure was pretty though – you know – brassy hair and freckles all over the place. I didn't love Karen like I did Ronnie, who wasn't my type at all. Love is like that, I suppose. You go around the world looking for the kind of girl that is your type – brassy hair and freckles all over the place – and then you lose your heart to someone who isn't your sort at all. I swear I'll never understand old *Mr Love* as long as I live.

Anyway, Karen hit a treble twenty on the dartboard and when I jumped up to congratulate her I banged my head in the doorway. Everything went black for a second and then sparks began to dribble across my eyes. The sparks got brighter and brighter until my mind exploded into about a million bits of light. They were like powdered stars. After that there was just darkness again and a loud hammering in my brain.

The first thing I saw when I came round was Karen and when I saw how frightened she looked it scared the hell out of me too. Karen said she thought I was dead or something worse. Apparently, according to Karen, I passed out on the floor for a few minutes and my body was twitching horribly. *For Chrissake Karen*, I said. Karen then went on to say that my eyes went into my head, so that they looked all white, and I started saying crazy things. I jawed at her that I was always saying crazy things. I was as well. I was always saying crazy things to make Karen laugh. I have to make everybody I meet laugh. It's so that they'll like me, I know. Listen, if they're laughing, they like me; if they're not, they don't.

So, anyway, I told Karen that I was always saying crazy things, talking like Americans and saying things like *Chrissake*. I reminded her it was the reason she damn well liked me in the first place. Karen laughed at everything I said until I said I love you and then she cried. I swear I'll never understand girls. All they do all day long is try and make themselves look pretty so that men will fall in love with them. It's the only thing on their minds, I'm telling you. It's like they can't help themselves or something. I think they're probably conditioned to act that way from birth. It sure makes me feel good though. I think I love girls just about more than anything on earth.

Anyway, I put a hand in my hair and it felt wet, and when I looked there was blood on my fingers. Listen to this next bit: *I felt sick to my heart*. Listen, you'd better know that I'm not too good at finding blood on my fingers like that. My head started swimming real bad. Everything was going black again. I thought I was dying for sure.

Then a few specks of wonderful light chipped holes in the blackness and it reminded me of the times we used to go to the

Lawn Cinema in Birstall. Sometimes, while you were watching a film, the screen would suddenly burn up in front of your eyes. It was all very dramatic, of course. Boy, we saw some great old films there though, didn't we Jenny? Do you remember when Mum took us to see *Bambi*? Jenny sat through the whole film without saying a word and I was going crazy with happiness. I couldn't take my eyes off Jenny and she couldn't take her eyes off the screen. Bambi was flicking his skinny legs all over the place and Thumper was smacking the ice so hard you thought it must break. I think Jenny loved Bambi more than anything else in the world. It sure was a sad film though. I tell you, when Bambi's mother died up there on the screen, I think I just about died along with her.

Anyway, after I saw the blood on my fingers I staggered into the living room and fell down on the sofa. I showed Jenny my hand and she immediately got down on the carpet and put her feet on the sofa. She said that if you put your feet higher than your head then you were guaranteed not to faint. Jenny's terrified about fainting. I swear she's worse about blood than I am. I laughed like an elk and then cried some because it made my head hurt worse than before. I thought I was going to die for sure. I thought I would die and the last thing I would see would be Jenny's feet next to my head.

Anyway, I didn't die. I felt much better all of a sudden. I jumped up. I wanted to open the front door and run about a thousand miles. I could have done it too, if only somebody had opened the door for me. That's how I felt. I could have run a million miles, but I didn't have the strength to open the front door. Karen started screaming. Jenny got up off the floor and ran upstairs. Karen had her hands over her ears for Chrissake. I told Karen to shut the hell up because she was making my head hurt worse. Jenny shouted down at me from the top of the stairs. She said that although she loved me and would do anything for me, she definitely wasn't coming back down until I'd washed the blood off my fingers. I laughed like an elk again at that. I told Jenny that she was just a cry-baby when all was said and done. We sure were having some fun with it all.

Karen was becoming hysterical. She begged me to stop talking to Jenny when we both knew she wasn't even there, and everything. She threatened to run out of the house if I didn't promise I couldn't see Jenny. I could see Jenny though. She was peeping at me through the banisters at the top of the stairs. Old Jenny was always peeping down at you from between the banisters until it just about drove you crazy.

I suddenly ran up the stairs hollering. I was holding my hand out so Jenny could see the blood again. She ran into her bedroom and slammed the door shut. Jenny was always slamming doors all over the place until they were just about falling off their hinges. I couldn't stop laughing. I was laughing when I put my head under the cold-water tap in the bathroom and I was laughing when the blood ran down the sink.

Then the awful thing happened: I looked out of the bathroom window and I suddenly wanted to die. I was done. Listen, I'd had enough of it, okay? It was something about the colour of the light. It was so awful white and the blood on the towel was so awful red. I wanted to get right down on the bathroom floor and die. And I did sit down on the bathroom floor, only I didn't die, I just shivered a whole load because it was cold. There wasn't really pain anymore, just a heavy feeling of sadness that I couldn't shake off. The thoughts inside my head were grinding to a halt. I think it was because Jenny was there when she shouldn't have been. I sat there for about an hour because I was too scared to go out of the door. I didn't want to find that Jenny was still there and I didn't want to find that she wasn't. Karen shouted up the stairs that she was leaving. She also said she never wanted to see me again. I didn't know whether to laugh or cry, so I cried. When I heard the front door slam I cried harder.

When I went downstairs Jenny was watching the television like nothing had happened. I sat down on the sofa next to her. I was still crying, for Chrissake. Jenny went into detail about why Karen had left. She never even turned her head to look at me. I felt real tired all of a sudden and knew that if I didn't lie down I would flake out. I closed my eyes and went to sleep for about a thousand years. I was a proper Rip Van Winkle, I admit it.

When I woke up it was dark in the room. I sat up. I felt cold and numb. My head was hurting like hell again. I called out to Karen and then remembered that she had gone. Jenny was still watching the television, but it was scary now because she hadn't turned the light on and the pictures were flickering like crazy on the walls. Jenny wasn't even on the sofa anymore. She was sitting directly in front of the television and I could only see the back of her head. She was so close to the television it must have been hurting her eyes. Jenny always sits too close to the television; she wears glasses, for Chrissake.

Anyway, I stretched my arm out from the sofa and let it sort of hang in the air behind Jenny's head. I started to cry again because it was all so terribly sad and everything. Listen, before we go any further, you'd better know that I'm always crying about something, okay? I can watch an advert on the television about house insurance and start crying. I think it was because Jenny's hair was so beautiful. I wanted to stroke it, but I didn't dare. I thought that, maybe, if I did, it would ruin everything. It was just about the most beautiful thing and when you see something like that you know you can't mess it up.

Jenny turned around, suddenly, and looked at me. She had a sweet smile on her face and it terrified me. The walls were dark, but the television flickered, like bright scratchy light, behind her head. Someone had turned the volume up real loud and my nerves were starting to get bad. The curtains were open and the streetlamp outside suddenly came on. I felt numb. I felt like I was slipping away.

"Hello funny face," Jenny said.

"Hello yourself," I said. "You shouldn't be here."

"I'm going to bed in a minute."

"You know what I mean."

"Who put you in charge?" she said, and pinched my nose.

"I mean it this time. And turn the television down. I'm the oldest here, okay?"

"Oh stop fussing. You're trying to sound like Daddy again."

Jenny pulled a face. Kids are like that. They can be smiling one minute, talking ten to the dozen, telling you what they did at school, and then the next minute they're telling you how much they hate you and never want to speak to you again.

"Does your head still hurt?" she said.

"Yes it does, little one."

"I didn't like seeing the blood on your fingers. It was mean of you to show me. I'm not good with blood am I?"

"No you're not," I said.

"Can I come and lie on the sofa next to you like I used to when I got really scared?"

"Yes. Why, are you scared now?"

"A little, what with all the excitement."

I shuffled over so that Jenny could lie next to me. I put my arm around her. She was soft and warm – and yes – it made me want to cry again.

"It's been a long time since we've done this," I said.

"Yes, I know."

I held her more tightly. "We should do this more often."

"I know, but things are different now."

"I wish things were like they used to be," I said.

"I know. We all do, of course we do, but they can't be. Not anymore. You've got to grow up now and start taking responsibility for your own life. Mummy and Daddy can't look after you for ever, you know."

"I suppose not."

"That's right. You're like a child, for Chrissake."

"Don't swear," I said.

"You make anyone swear. I swear you do."

I laughed a little and then stroked her hair.

"You always laugh when people are trying to tell you something important," she said. "Why do you do that? Why won't you listen to the people who love you most?"

"Where did all that come from? Who's trying to sound like the parent now? You're only a child when all is said and done."

"Oh you make me want to scream. Why can't you ever take things seriously? You're hopeless, you really are."

"Smelly bum," I sniggered.

"Oh, you're incorrigible, you really are. Nobody thinks you're being funny, you know."

"Why are you laughing then?"

"Because you always could make me laugh."

"I know. Please don't stop laughing until I'm asleep. I don't think I could bear it."

I fell asleep to the sound of Jenny laughing and when I woke up the next morning she was gone.

2

A few weeks after I hit my head I finished with Karen.

She came to my house one morning and I just told her we were through. I told her this while she stood freezing on the doorstep, waiting to come into the house. She looked pretty though and a part of me regretted it. Karen hit the roof. She said she hoped I dropped dead or something. I shut the door in her face because I'm not good with confrontation, but she started yelling it all through the letter-box. She said she hated me and had never really wanted to go out with me in the first place. I said I didn't blame her one iota. Karen said her mum thought I was probably neurotic or something. Then she started crying and begged me to take her back. I said I jolly well wouldn't take her back and went and lay down on my bed. In the end I had to put a pillow over my head so I couldn't hear her anymore.

I got over Karen pretty quickly. I'm like that. I pretty much fall in love with a girl a few seconds after meeting her. I tell girls things I know they'll love, like they fill my world and I can't breathe when I'm near them. All kinds of stuff like that. Believe it when I tell you that they can never resist me for too long. For a while I think they're the happiest they've ever been. Then I lose interest all of a sudden. I break their hearts, I think. Jenny said you break a girl's heart when you finish with her. I never feel bad when I break up with girls though. I just feel relieved it's all over. Jenny said that one day when I really fall in love I'll be the one who gets my heart broken. I love it when Jenny gets worked up about breaking girls' hearts like that.

Anyway, I left my parents' home and got a room in the city. I took all my savings from the bank and just went one morning. Mum didn't speak much, but she made me breakfast. When I went outside it was grey and rainy. I got a room above the Angel Gateway. The Angel Gateway is a strange little alleyway that runs between Gallowtree Gate and the market. It sounds beautiful but isn't. In fact, it's just about the most depressing place you'll ever see. I love all that beautiful-sounding-name stuff for places that are as depressing as hell, don't you? I really get off on that sort of thing.

I got real low that first day alone in my new room. It was a Sunday and because Sundays always bothered me I went for a stroll along New Walk. New Walk's about a hundred miles long and my dad used to live there when he was a kid. It's all very serene down there and the houses are so pretty they make you want to get down on the ground and cry.

It felt strange standing outside Dad's old house. I was trying to guess which room he'd slept in when I saw an old woman looking out of a window at me. I think she was surprised to see me standing outside her house like that. I smiled and waved a little to try and smooth things over. I tried to tell her it was the house where my dad was born. I said it too quietly though – like you do when you're talking to people behind glass – and she didn't hear me. I raised my voice a little until I was practically shouting. I tried to tell her everything would be okay; it was just my dad's old house. I didn't want her to think I was just some random lunatic or something. She suddenly put her hands over her face and burst into tears. It must be pretty awful having somebody screaming outside your house like that. I said I was sorry and left.

I was bored, I admit it. I was missing Jenny so much I decided to go to the museum to see Daniel Lambert's chair. Jenny loved to sit in Daniel Lambert's chair and flick her legs out all over the place. Old Danny boy was so fat you could get a hundred kids on that chair. And behind the chair, pinned on the wall, was a pair of Danny's trousers. I swear they were about a mile wide. Listen, Daniel Lambert was pretty much Leicester's favourite son back in the good old days.

Danny was a gaoler and used to fight bears in the street. He weighed about a hundred and fifty stone at one point and was the fattest man in the world. Honest to God, old Danny boy once knocked a bear clean out. Apparently, some crazy old American grizzly came to Leicester and killed Danny's favourite dog, and old Danny boy was so upset he socked it on the muzzle and knocked it out cold. Listen, Danny boy was also just about the strongest man in the world back then too, okay?

Anyway, in his later life, Danny boy became a bit of a recluse. He wouldn't come out of his room because he was so ashamed of his weight, which is pretty funny really because that was the reason he became famous in the first place. And, apparently, some feller once went to Danny's room to ask him a question about cock-fighting. You see, old Danny knew more about cock-fighting than anyone else in the world and this feller, who was a really important lord or something, by all accounts, wanted to ask Danny's advice about some minor detail. Well, old Danny boy told his servant to tell this important feller that he wouldn't see him because he was a "shy cock" himself.

Anyway, old Danny got so lonely and poor he had to join a circus to make ends meet. Old Danny boy was really coining it in by all accounts because the good people of Leicester just wanted to come and shake his big goddamn fat hand. Daniel hated the fact he was making money out of the thing he despised most about himself though. Danny was just about the shyest man in the world back then and talking about his weight made him want to crawl away and hide. Listen, this guy had some kind of chronic social phobia or something, okay?

People were always asking Danny what size clothes he wore until it just about made him sick with humiliation. And once, some wise guy asked him how big his trousers were and Danny boy said that if the man went out and brought him a pair then he would know how big they were. Danny boy said it in a real cool way as well by all accounts. It really made me howl when I heard that old Danny had said it like that.

Anyway, when I got to the museum I found you couldn't sit on Danny boy's chair like you used to; somebody had hung some rope across it. His trousers were still pinned on the wall, but I didn't have the heart to stay long. It made me all very depressed again. I hoped that Jenny wouldn't find out about the rope because I knew it would just about break her heart.

So I left the museum and went to see the Jewry Wall. I watched sparrows pecking the grass. I felt awful and wanted to die again like the time in the bathroom. I stayed there for most of the day staring at the wall and the sparrows. Eventually the sparrows left and I was the only one there. I was the saddest person in the whole world by then, I guess. I stayed there so long I saw the streetlamps come on. They glimmered in the gloom like a row of pearls or something. I don't know. Maybe I'm just getting carried away by things. It started to rain, a sorrowful rain; the kind of black rain that goes straight through your clothes to your heart. The light from the streetlamps reflected on the wet pavements next to the grass and I heaved with sickness. It was all pretty tragic when you think about it.

I used to lie in bed with my hands over my mouth so I wouldn't scream. I wanted to scream so badly some nights it was terrifying and the only way I could stop myself was to bite my fingers. I had an unhealthy compulsion around that time to run down the street and scream in people's faces. I think I wanted them to be terrified too. It was scary because you know that as soon as you do it you're finished. Once you start screaming there's no going back. I mean it. Once you give in to it, you're through, because all those people who never noticed you before suddenly will notice you. And the doctors won't leave you alone for the rest of your life. Listen, I'm telling you for your own good. Don't scream, okay?

I used to sit on my bed reading. I must have read about a million books back then. I spent whole days in the Black Cat Bookshop. I can read pretty fast when I'm scared. I read feverishly, I think. No listen, it's true, I can read through the night. It's because I don't sleep too good I know.

I read a book about this guy who was a comedian. It all

happened about a million years ago in the good old days of variety entertainment and everything. Apparently, this comedian was just about the funniest guy on the planet back then. I think his name was Charlie Cheeky Boy, or something, I don't know, I can't remember. Anyway, old Charlie had the audience eating out of his goddamn hands he was so funny. He also wore just about the brightest suit you ever saw. I know this because there was a photograph of him and, although it was in black and white, you just knew the suit was real loud by the pattern.

Listen, there's another thing you should know about Charlie, okay? *He was risqué.* Listen, this guy was blue. He used to tickle the ladies' fancies back then until they were practically begging him to sleep with them. I don't know, perhaps I made that bit about sleeping with him up. Listen, this chap could make the audiences of today blush. He was bubbly, believe me.

Anyway – and here's the important bit, the part that I couldn't get out of my mind – this cheeky chappie, this wise-guy who was always rolling his eyes at the ladies on stage, was chronically shy off it. I swear he was. Listen to me. It was all in the book, okay? This impostor couldn't even hold a proper conversation with you he was so inept socially. Christ, this bloke couldn't even look you in the eye, for Chrissake. The book said that this so-called hotshot had some kind of social phobia. Boy, I just couldn't take it in too well. This charlatan just stayed in his room all day because he was terrified of going out and meeting people.

He never had any friends. In fact, the author couldn't find one person in the whole damn world who actually knew the guy personally. Christ, all those women screaming at him and he never once had a girlfriend. Listen, he never had a sexual experience in his life. Behind all that laughter, this guy was nothing. He was a one-trick fucking pony and it just about killed me to read about it, okay? You take the laughter away and there's nothing. It's all in the book.

3

Anyway, I met this really nice girl called Ronnie. Ronnie wasn't just a nice girl, she was *the* girl – you know – the girl you finally meet and fall in love with. I think I fell in love with Ronnie about a split-second after I first saw her. Listen, Ronnie wasn't the most beautiful girl in the world or anything, but she sure was pretty. She had long black hair cascading down her back – yes, cascading – and grey eyes that just about took your breath away. Sometimes, if Ronnie laid her eyes on you without warning, you were done for. One second you were staring at her, thinking she didn't know, and the next second, wham, she'd turn around and look at you. There was no warning, believe me. There were white flecks in Ronnie's eyes that lit up brighter than chalk strokes on a blackboard, and that's me being romantic. Ronnie's eyes could throw you around the room, if you let them. And I think Ronnie knew the effect her eyes had on you, if you really want to know. I think Ronnie did all that eye-flicking stuff on purpose. I think it used to amuse her when all was said and done. Yeah, thinking about it, I reckon old Ronnie was bursting with pride because she knew damn well she could get the whole male population down on their knees if she wanted to.

Ronnie's skin was so white it made you go blind if you looked at her too long. It was that white. It made you rub your eyes like you'd got a welding flash or something. It was like Jenny suddenly bursting into your bedroom at night and turning on the light. Boy, didn't Jenny sure get a kick out of doing that? She'd stand there laughing while you were trying to throw your pillow at her and missing, for Chrissake, because you couldn't keep your eyes open long enough to aim it. Jenny used to shriek like a madwoman, dancing on the heels of her feet and waving her skinny arms around, practically begging you to get out of bed and chase her back to her own room. God bless you, Jenny. Anyway, old Ronnie's skin was brighter than a light that is switched on suddenly, when you're half asleep and it's dark in your room.

Ronnie sure had just about the perfect body too. She wasn't too fat and she wasn't too skinny. Some girls are so skinny they make you want to throw up all over them. They look so damn sickly and everything; it bothers me, okay? Listen, I'm just about the shallowest person you're ever going to meet, okay? I'm not proud of it, of course I'm not, but I probably won't even talk to you if you're ugly. Listen, you'd better understand that if you're real gruesome and you start trying to strike up a conversation with me, I'm very likely going to just walk away from you. I might even run, okay?

You might be just about the cleverest person in the world, maybe even a goddamn genius like Stephen Hawking, or something, I don't know, and you might be trying to tell me all about how the universe started, and everything, but if you're ugly, that's all I'm going to see. You could be on the verge of telling me the secret of life and I'm still going to run away from you before you've finished. You could have a solution to world hunger; I don't care, because listen, I'm still going, okay? I sure hate myself for being so damn shallow sometimes.

Anyway, I think I really messed things up badly that first time I tried to talk to Ronnie. I think she thought I was some kind of mental case or something. I can laugh about it now, of course I can, but it wasn't funny back then. It was my own fault entirely, I admit it. I tried too crazy hard to make her laugh. I was hoping she would love me back, of course. Sometimes young girls just don't want to hear all that crazy stuff, especially when they're working on Leicester market and the boss is looking over their shoulder.

Well, this is how it happened: I was strolling around the market one day – casually if you must know – when I saw her and I just about got down on my knees and cried. I was smashed by her. It felt like my heart detonated inside of me, or something. Dizzy? Let me tell you about dizzy. I swear the ground was moving so fast I had to grab hold of a stall to stop myself from falling. My eyes were crawling all over her. (Hey, I'm not proud of that, okay?) My poor head was spinning so much I thought I was in a spin-dryer. I stood looking at her for about a hundred years or more.

I started humming love songs, real loud too, hoping that she would hear me. I was trying to impress her, I guess. And she did hear me because she kind of glanced over in my direction. She was trying to see where all the gorgeous tunes were coming from. After about a million years I plucked up the courage to say a few words to her. You know, break the ice a little, chew the fat, and get to know her.

Anyway, it started well enough, but then it got out of hand, unravelled away from me, if you like. Listen, if you're trying to sell fruit to the nation and some lame-brained mental case tries to strike up a conversation with you, it stands to reason you're going to get annoyed about it, okay? I understand that now, of course I do, but I didn't understand it then. If you're trying to shovel fruit into the bag of Customer A, you're going to be pretty annoyed if Customer B (i.e. me) is trying to make you fall in love with them.

Anyway, I tried to strike up a conversation with her.

"Say, what's your name, fruit lady?"

As soon as I said it I knew it was a mistake because she gave me a real sour look.

"Are you talking to me?" she snapped.

"Of course, love of my life. So, what's your name, pretty one?"

I looked away as I said it and yawned. I was trying to look bored. Romantically I was at my best.

"Ronnie. What's yours?"

When she told me her name was Ronnie she wasn't even looking at me anymore. She'd started serving customers again and it annoyed me a little, to tell you the truth, even though I knew it was her job and everything. Her boss was already starting to hang around in the background. He was cleaning his teeth with a matchstick.

Anyway, I started it up again. I was love-struck, I admit it.

"Ronnie? Say, isn't that a man's name?"

I said it with a damn fine twinkle in my eye too because girls love that sort of thing.

Ronnie didn't answer me, but I loved her anyway. I think she didn't answer me because she didn't realise I was still talking to her. I'd said it all too quietly, more to myself really. It was also because she was busy shuffling potatoes into someone's bag and messing it up pretty badly, if you want to know, because some of them rolled on to the ground. I was sure sore as hell that she'd missed the twinkle in my eye.

"I said isn't that a man's name or something?"

I shouted it the second time and about as loud as I could so that she would hear me.

"Sorry?"

She did hear me. Christ, I think everybody heard me. Her boss sure as hell heard me because he started giving me the daggers.

Ronnie looked like she hated my guts or something. I think she was a little annoyed because she'd dropped the potatoes on the floor and the customer had yelled at her as if they were diamonds or something. Customers can get really worked up about those things. Believe me, I know. Listen, even my mum can get pretty sore at somebody if they don't put the potatoes into her bag well enough, okay?

"Ronnie! Isn't that a man's name? *For Chrissake.*" I said it real quietly again the third time. I was shaking by then, I admit it.

Ronnie looked at me as if I'd gone off my head, bless her. I gave her my best smile – you know – the one that Jenny says I use when I want to get my own way. My eyes were twinkling again as well. I'm like that. I can just switch it on whenever the mood takes me. I can be as miserable as death one minute and then start with the twinkling eyes and dashing smiles the next.

Jenny said you can't be normal if you can change your moods as quickly as that. I told her you get used to it.

"My name's Veronica, but people call me Ronnie. Is there something you want, sir?"

I think she said it loud like that, and called me sir, because her boss was standing behind her. Ronnie sure seemed to be looking over her shoulder about a million times when she said it.

"Yes, there is something else. I want to take you by the hand and then run, laughing, to the old Clock Tower and back. Then I want to kiss you on the mouth and marry you."

Where this gem came from I don't know, but I was pretty damn proud of it, I can tell you. Girls love all that kind of thing. Believe me, I know. My eyes were twinkling so much by then they could have lit up the whole damn city. My mouth was starting to hurt because I was smiling so hard. I was practically grinning like a clown in front of her. The sweat was dripping down my face from the exertion. It was all worth it though. I mean, when you're trying to win the girl of your dreams you've got to pull out all the stops. And believe me, I always do. I have to try so hard it just about tears me in two.

Then Ronnie half smiled and it just about pushed me over. In fact, it just about cleared me out, if you really want to know. It also depressed me because I knew I'd never see that smile again. Sure, I figured there'd be other smiles, but never that first one. I was starting to get choked up about the whole thing. I didn't want to dwell on it too long.

"Are you alright?" said Ronnie.

"No, I'm not," I said.

I wasn't either. I don't think you ever get over something like that easily.

"Listen, is there something you want to buy because we're pretty busy *and my boss is looking?*"

Old Ronnie whispered the last part so that her boss wouldn't hear her. She also came a bit nearer to my face when she said it and I almost shouted. People like Ronnie should warn you before they move their face up close like that.

"Listen, Veronica, Ronnie, say, were you named after Ronnie Spector from The Ronettes? Hey, I sure as hell hope you were because I love The Ronettes. I love that song, 'Be My Baby'. Christ, Ronnie, please say you were named after Ronnie Spector, so that I don't have to just crawl away and die somewhere. Say, how do you fancy going out walking with me?"

Christ, I sure as hell was pleased with that line. It sure sounded all romantic, and everything, like in the olden days when our parents went courting. I bet my mum went out walking with my dad. God, I kind of felt sorry for old Ronnie, what with all the gorgeous lines I was laying down and my eyes twinkling like goddamn stars or something.

Poor Ronnie never stood a chance from the start.

"Are you a nutcase or something?" she said.

Good old Ronnie; she sure was playing it cool and hard-to-get. Hey listen, I can play it cool too, okay, so I told her about the bang on the head.

"Listen, Ronnie, R.O.N.N.I.E. S.P.E.C.T.O.R., say will you 'Be My Baby'? No, listen, only kidding. I am a little crazy to be honest. I had a bit of a bang to the old head a few weeks ago, but I'm alright now. *I'm not alright.* I'm feeling as right as rain now, it's just that I get so sad and depressed all the time. I'm lonely, okay, deal with it. No, I get real low sometimes – *all the time* – sinking to the bottom of the sea and then not being able to swim back up. Can't quite manage to reach the surface, if you see what I mean old fruit, old fruit lady? I can see the sky behind the sea, but I can't manage to get to it. Boy, where did all that come from? I reckon I've eaten so much fruit I've turned into a fruit loop. Or a fruit man. Hey, fruit lady, can I be your fruit man? Please God, let me be your fruit man."

Boy, I was breathing like I'd just run up a mountain or something. I was sweating like a horse.

"Are you weak in the head?" said Ronnie.

"Yes, and strong in the arm." I showed Ronnie the muscles on my arms. "No, listen, Ronnie, I'm pretty weak most of the time these days because that's how you make me feel."

"You're crazy."

"Jenny said I make her laugh."

I was desperate.

She ran away from me.

I didn't feel too well all of a sudden. I wanted someone to take me home, I suppose. Hearing myself speaking like that had shaken me up a little.

I could see Ronnie talking to her boss across the other side of the stall. She was telling him about me for sure. What hurt most was the frightened look on her face. It really tore me up, if you want to know the truth. I started to cry a little, I think. I wasn't well, I admit it.

Then Ronnie came back and said people like me should be locked up. I told her that was a pretty cruel thing to say, when all is said and done, and especially to someone who obviously wasn't well. Then her frigging boss came from behind the stall and poked me so hard in the chest I nearly fell over. I decided to get away from there pretty quick. Listen, don't believe what they try to tell you. Romance is dead, okay?

I went and sat down by the fountain. Girls can be so cruel sometimes. Ronnie, I mean. I was feeling lousy and my head was hurting. Everything inside was turning black again. It was because I was in love with Ronnie, I know. Listen, when those feelings come around there pretty well isn't much you can do about it.

I watched the water smash like glass on the ground. I was kind of hoping that Jenny was with me and we were kids again. God, I think they were just about the happiest days of my life. I started wishing that Jenny could still be frightened by the water, but I knew she wouldn't be. Listen, I didn't want Jenny to be the sort of person who isn't half scared to death when the water from the fountain smashes on the ground, okay?

There is a poem by old Wendell Holmes that we read at school. There are only two lines I remember:

"A few can touch the magic string, and noisy Fame is proud to win them:- Alas for those that never sing, but die with all their music in them!"

It sure used to make me feel sad when we read those lines. I think it's tragic that a hell of a lot of people die with their music still inside them.

Listen, it doesn't matter if you sing your song and it's terrible, okay? It doesn't matter one iota. All that matters is that you try and sing it. If it's lousy, that's okay. You can live with lousy. For Chrissake, just give it your best shot, won't you? If you don't at least try to sing your song you won't be able to live with yourself. It will eat you up inside and you'll regret it for the rest of your life. There will always be a deep unhappiness inside you no matter how hard you're trying to convince the world that there isn't. And you don't know, it might just be the most beautiful song they've ever heard. God, I think it's really tragic if people don't at least try and sing their goddamn song and all.

I don't know what old Wendell Holmes meant by *the magic string*, but I think he meant trying to grab hold of the thing that you want most in life. Yeah, I'm convinced that's what he meant. He's telling us - in his own poetic way, of course - that only a very few are lucky enough to get hold of their own *magic string*. It's because they never sing the song that is bursting inside them. I hope to God I don't die without touching *the magic string* and all. I know I probably won't get hold of it - but Christ - you've got to at least try, haven't you?

And that's why I knew I had to go back and try all over again with Ronnie. I reckon I knew she was my *magic string* and it was fucking crucial I tried to sing the song inside me again. I almost did as well.

Look, I just don't get on with people too well, okay? I don't let people get too close. This sounds tragic, I know, but I find it a whole lot easier to walk into a room full of strangers than I do walking into a room full of people I know. I can't afford to stay too long in one place because they'll discover I'm nothing special. I've got to tell you about a thousand jokes an hour to keep you laughing because I know that as soon as I stop, it's over for me. I'm terrified that once I stop you'll see I'm ordinary. I can't stay in one place for too long. I've got to lay down some magic pretty quickly – normally within the first few minutes – and then I've got to get the hell out of there while you're still dazzled. I've got to leave you thinking that the memory of me was a lot more special than the real thing. I swear I just can't keep it going for too long, okay? Once my tired routine is finished, and everyone is talking about the normal stuff again, I'm done for.

Listen, if you ever meet me – and I hope you do – you're going to think I'm a real funny guy. But when the laughter stops you're going to see one sad individual. I don't want you to see that person, okay, so it's better that I get the hell away from you as quickly as possible. I'll break my heart to make you laugh. Believe me, I really will. I'm ready to get down and die in front of you just to make you smile. If you're laughing then everything's okay; if you're not laughing then everything's not okay. It's all pretty tragic when you analyse it. And believe me, I have. About a million times already.

Pretty soon, young man, you'll be the only one who notices the person with the frightened look in their eyes. Look, that person with the frightened look in their eyes is me, okay, and I sure as hell don't want you to have to see him. I don't want to put you through it. It's chronic really. It sure must be the most embarrassing thing in the world: watching a person struggle like that. I feel real sorry for you. Listen, I can't do it any differently, okay? I've tried about a million times, but I can't deliver. I swear I want to be normal, like everybody else, but it's a no go, I'm afraid. I'm virtually begging you all to love me.

So I left the fountain and went and stood on the edge of the market again. I was on the outside looking in. I knew that, of course I did. I stayed there for an hour or two, trying to catch

Ronnie's eye. I love all that catching girls' eyes stuff, don't you? I'm just a flirt at heart, I suppose. I love to give girls the eye and then flirt with them a little so that they think they've got a chance with me. Then I love to let them down all of a sudden. Listen, one moment I'm going to be fooling around with you – trying to break your goddamn heart and everything – and then the next minute I probably won't even look at you. Christ, I won't even speak to you if you're not careful. And it's probably breaking my heart a lot more than it is yours, okay? Listen, it's probably a lot easier to break my heart than you think.

I used to get pretty lonely in my room, but I think I already told you that. Jenny used to come and visit me sometimes, but she could never stay long because we both knew that she shouldn't have been there. She used to sit checking her watch about fifty times an hour until I just about begged her to go home, for Chrissake. I sure as hell missed her after she'd gone though.

It's funny, one minute I couldn't leave the room because I was too scared to go outside and the next minute I had to get out before I went crazy. Honestly, that's how it was. I used to walk around all day just to have something to do. I just kept walking. I really did. I couldn't stop myself. I was like a goddamn marathon walker or something. I think I must have walked to the moon and back during that time. I was scared of stopping because I knew I'd probably start screaming if I did. The panic was always there, just a few inches in front of my face, and I knew the only way I could stop it was to keep walking. Sometimes I had to walk about a hundred miles I was so terrified. I knew that if I stopped, I was finished.

4

I woke up one morning and needed to see my dad. It was cold in my room and I knew that Dad was the strongest person in the whole world back then. I wanted to tell him about the screaming because I figured that if anyone could make the feelings stop, he could. Listen, when I was a kid I thought my dad was frigging Hercules or something, okay? I thought he could beat just about everybody in the whole world back then, including Sonny Liston. My dad could move goddamn mountains if he wanted to. I sure as hell was a disappointment to him.

I went back to my home village and found Dad sitting at a table by himself in his favourite pub. He was staring at a glass of beer in front of him. He looked like the saddest person I ever saw. I knew pretty much straight away that he couldn't help me because he had enough pain of his own. I knew he was thinking about Jenny. Hell, we were all thinking about Jenny.

When Dad lifted his head up I couldn't tell whether he was pleased or disappointed to see me. I was trying my hardest to look cute, but he looked straight through me. His eyes looked awful blurry and tired. I sure wanted to hug him all of a sudden, but I knew that was impossible. I always have to work twice as hard to please my dad. I suddenly wished Ronnie was there too because I desperately needed her to see what a real man looked like. I wanted her to fall in love with him like every other girl in the world did.

"Hello Dad," I said cheerfully; it sounded ghastly.

"Hello son," he said.

"It sure is good to see you again. Take the pain away, won't you?"

I felt pretty bad afterwards – you know – asking him to take away the pain so quickly like that, especially when he was so deeply troubled himself.

"Let me get you a drink," he said. I don't think he heard the bit about taking the pain away.

"Gee, thanks, Dad, I'll have a soda pop."

I sure don't know what I was thinking – you know – talking in a silly high-pitched voice like that, like I was still a child, or something, and asking for a soda pop, for Chrissake.

"What the hell is a soda pop?"

"I've no idea, Dad."

"For Chrissake, have a proper drink. Have a beer, alright?"

I just nodded. I could never get it right with him.

When Dad came back from the bar he put the drink down in front of me. Then we both stared at it for about eleven days or something. We never said a word. In the end I drank some of the beer, just to have something to do, and shivered, and then nearly died because it tasted so cold and awful.

Dad started the father and son bit. You know the sort of thing. Telling me about the facts of life and all that other crap. He kept asking if everything was okay and I just nodded, and felt uncomfortable, and took another sip of my beer, and then nearly died again because it still tasted so foul. I knew it wasn't the right time to tell Dad about screaming and wondered how I was going to get away.

I sure as hell felt a fraud sitting there, I can tell you. Listen, you'd better understand that when a dad and his son have a drink in the pub they should talk about how well Leicester City football team is doing. There should be no mention of screaming at all because something like that is really going to ruin the party atmosphere. Your old dad wants to hear that his son is doing just fine, and everything, and that he's got the best job in the world, and everybody at work thinks he's a swell kind of guy. Your father does not want to hear that you're scared to death and might start screaming any day soon. Your dad wants to hear that you're just about the most popular kid around and that everybody is just bending over backwards to be in your groovy gang. Listen, Dad, nobody wants to be in my gang, okay?

Then I did something really stupid and it was only because I was feeling so crummy and nervous, and everything, I know.

I picked up my beer mat and ripped it into small pieces. Then I placed them down on the table in front of him. I'd made a little building, for Chrissake. Dad looked mortified and I didn't blame him one iota. He put his beer glass down for a second and looked at me for a thousand years. I couldn't hold his stare though and just gazed down at the ruined pieces of beer mat like they were bits of ripped-up human flesh or something. I felt so ashamed of those bits of torn-up beer mat, suddenly, and I wanted to collect them together and hide them. My dad sure makes me feel nervous all the time, I can tell you. I just can't relax in his company, I swear it.

Anyway, I just sort of ran my trembling fingers through the pieces of beer mat for a few seconds. Then I sat back in the chair, folded my arms tightly and tried to make it look like I'd never seen them before. I tried to look like I didn't know who the hell had done it, but it certainly wasn't me, okay? Dad continued to look at me, but I couldn't look back at him for all the tea in China. All I could do was stare at the pieces of beer mat arranged in between us. I felt something near to disgust when I looked at them.

"What did you do that for?" Dad finally said.

"Sorry?" I said, without looking up at him.

"This is a pub. People are looking at you. Don't you care that they think there's something wrong with you?"

"Is that what they think, Dad?"

"You don't come into a pub and start tearing up your beer mat."

"Don't you?" I said it quietly.

"What's wrong with you? Why do you do things like that?"

"Sorry, Dad," I said.

I was so sorry by then I think I started to cry or something. I sure was sniffing loudly.

"Don't cry, for Chrissake." Dad started looking around the bar.

"Sorry, Dad."

"Don't keep apologising. Just stop crying. Drink your beer, for crying out loud."

"I don't like it. It's too strong."

"Fucking hell."

Dad sagged in his seat and shook his head. Then he let out

a long sigh and rubbed his tired, yellow eyes. He looked ruined – like the beer mat – and I felt pretty awful about things. It just about cleared me out, if you really want to know. Then he lowered his head and looked down at the floor.

"Don't do that, Dad." My hand sort of hovered around his head for a few seconds, like I was going to stroke his hair or something.

Anyway – luckily – by the time Dad looked up my hand was safely in my lap. Listen, you'd better understand that your dad really doesn't want you to stroke his head tenderly like that, especially when you're both drinking in the pub and you're on a good night out, for Chrissake.

Well, Dad just stared at me for about a million more years. There was a hell of a lot of staring going on that day, I can tell you, and most of it was coming from Dad. Then he started chewing the ends of his fingers until I could virtually see the bone. Listen, my dad chews his fingernails too much, okay? My dad's fingers always look real sore and I'd hate myself if I thought I was the reason why.

"How are you feeling?" he said suddenly, so that it made me start. "You look terrible. You look like death warmed up. You keep blinking your eyes. Stop blinking your eyes. People are watching you. Can't you just be normal?"

I sure felt sorry for blinking my eyes like that in front of Dad. We were in a public bar, for Chrissake.

"Sorry, Dad," I said.

"Don't keep saying sorry. Just don't blink. Do you know why you do it?"

"I don't know. I really don't. When somebody tells me to

stop – i.e. you – I just kind of have to do it more. I do it more when you're here because I know it drives you crazy and all. I know it must be hard on you watching me show myself up in public like this."

"Just don't do it. Why is it every time I'm with you in a public place I've got to whisper?"

"I don't know the answer to that, sir, I really don't. It sure is something I'm going to think about though. I'm going to figure the answer to that one out and get right back to you."

Poor old Dad picked up his pint and finished it off in one manly swallow. His hands were shaking badly, but I didn't mention it out of politeness.

"You'd better go," he said.

"Okay, Dad. Sorry."

Anyway, after all the drama of seeing Dad, I went back to the market and tried to sing my song again. Ronnie saw me coming through the crowds though. I know she did because she went directly to her boss. She did not "Pass Go" and she did not "Collect £200". Ronnie's boss just stood there cleaning his teeth with a matchstick, for Chrissake. As Ronnie was speaking to him he kept looking over at me and nodding like he was weighing up quite a few things. It looked to me like he was contemplating something. When Ronnie had finished talking he walked out from behind the stall and came towards me. Listen, if you have a matchstick between your teeth it makes you look pretty tough, okay? I waved at him to ease the situation, but he didn't even crack a smile. I was determined though. I knew I was going to try and sing my song again, no matter what.

It sure seemed to take Ronnie's boss a long time to reach me. I had plenty of time to stand and watch Ronnie. Boy, but did she look pretty that day. The light shining through the cracks in the market roof lit her face up in the most delightful way. Beyond the market hall, rain sparkled in bright gaps. It was a beautiful thing. I'm convinced of it. I could hear music from somewhere. I think it was from the CD stall behind me. Ronnie's dark eyes glittered like beads and her mouth was nervous in a way I liked. I wanted her to be tough – of course I did – but I also wanted her to have a sweet side. If she hasn't got all that fear and tenderness in her eyes, well, it's just not worth it. Not in my book anyway. Not in the long run.

Well, I moved in for the kill, but Ronnie's boss cut me off at the pass. From being about a thousand miles away he was suddenly right in front of me. He was so near, in fact, I could have pulled the match out of his mouth with my own teeth. I could smell him too. He smelled of fruit. He was the real fruit man, not me.

"Listen, buster," he snarled. "Clear off."

That nearly killed me. Calling me buster like that as if we were in a gangster film or something. I was shaking like a madman though. It was all pretty intimidating, if you really want to know. He was like some crazy James Dean or something. I really hate all that macho confrontation stuff, don't you? I thought he was going to take the match out of his mouth and strike it on my clean, white, innocent throat.

"James Dean was gay, you know."

It was a cheap shot even for me.

"Scram."

"I forgot my fruit yesserday," I drawled.

I was trying to act like an American gangster myself or something. I kill myself sometimes, saying things like yesserday instead of yesterday. Listen, I warned you I can be a pretty funny guy when I want to.

"Okay, buster, just buy your fruit and clear off. And don't start any of that crazy stuff again. I don't want you scaring my staff, okay?"

It made me laugh a little more when he said "my staff" like that, like he had about a million people working for him. We both knew damn well that Ronnie was the only person who ever helped him out. Anyway, I told him I wouldn't disturb all his staff, I just wanted to buy some goddamn fruit for the weekend, if that was alright.

So anyway, I wandered, real casual, up to the stall and Ronnie started eyeing me up and down like I was a bleeding murderer or something. I started to examine the fruit on sale like I was a connoisseur from Del Monte or something. It was all just a game really. Ronnie asked me real politely if there was anything I wanted, and I sort of went along with it and pointed to different types of fruit I reckoned I might need for the weekend, and old Ronnie started putting them carefully into a bag, and eyeing me real suspiciously at the same time as if she thought I might explode at any moment.

And I was doing well, really well, and old James Dean was happily sucking his match at the back of the stall again. Things were back to normal. Ronnie's boss shouted over to Ronnie that he was going to fetch a cup of tea because it was so damn cold. I wanted to shout back that if he did a bit more work then he might warm up a little. He didn't even ask Ronnie if she wanted a drink, for Chrissake.

Anyway, after he'd gone I sort of lost it again. You know, thinking about the song and the magic string, and everything, and how I might as well try to get hold of it before it floated out of my life forever.

"So, do you come here often?" I said. I was just warming things up, if you like.

"What?"

Ronnie looked scared and it shook me a little.

"Oh just shut up and kiss me, you crazy fool," I said.

I switched my twinkling eyes back on and old Ronnie got the full, dazzling effect.

"Don't start all that nonsense again, okay? I'm warning you this time."

"You cut me to the quick, you know?" I tried to sound all wounded. I was all wounded, I admit it.

"Is there anything you want?"

"What sayeth you, fair maiden, would you care to ride with me upon my trusty white steed?"

I was sure playing up to the camera. She must have thought I was really out to impress her with all that trusty white steed stuff.

"Don't start all that mental crap with me again, okay?"

"Listen, Ronnie, old sport, old fruit, why don't we just cut to the chase? Throw down your fruit and let's get married like they did in the good old days before the war. What war? I don't know. Any war. Let's just do it anyway. Just me and you and a dog name Boo. And Jenny, of course. Jenny loves a church wedding more than anything in the world."

"Please go away," she said.

Ronnie sure sounded sore about something.

"I will only go away with you."

"Are you sick?"

"Sick with love," I whimpered.

I picked up an apple for some reason as if that were the only way to prove something like that. Love had got me all confused, I admit it.

"Geoff will be back any minute and he won't be too happy if he finds you're still here."

I think Geoff was her boss. I must admit, I sure as hell hated old Geoff at that moment. What with Ronnie saying his name all familiar like that, and not mine.

"My name's Arthur," I said.

"Hello Arthur," said Ronnie. She sure didn't sound too friendly when she said it either.

Boy, did I make a big mistake. My name's not even Arthur. My name's Franklin. I'm always doing that. Saying my name's Arthur, or something, when it isn't. I must think it's clever or something. It's not clever though, because now Ronnie would always call me Arthur, and not Franklin, and I'd never hear her say my real name. I thought about telling her that my name wasn't Arthur, it was Franklin, but I didn't want her to think I was some kind of mental case or something.

"Arthur and Ronnie," I said, rolling my eyes some. "Sounds like a match made in heaven."

"It sounds more like a tragedy," said Ronnie.

"Hey, you're funny. No really, do you love me yet?"

"Why do you talk so loud? You're just about shouting."

"You know me, I shoot from the lip. I'll shout it from the rooftops if you want?"

I got down on one knee. Boy, it sure was wet and cold down on the ground and all.

"Where are your parents? Do they know you're out on your own like this?"

"They lock me up, but I escape each night and run back to you."

"Get up, it's wet down there. There's fruit all over your trousers, you great nit."

I stood up. Ronnie was right. There was indeed a great wet patch on my trousers.

"Why don't you go home?" Ronnie said, more tenderly than before. "Before Geoff gets back and sees that you're still here."

"Your heart is my home now."

Boy, my knee sure did feel all messy and cold.

"Do you know what my favourite book is?" I said.

"I don't care."

"It's *A Padded Room with a View*. Only kidding, of course. I joke around a lot really. I have to joke about the serious things. It's the only way I can say them, I suppose. I can't say the serious things in a serious way. It's a tragedy, I know."

"You're the tragedy," she said. "I feel sorry for you."

I reached down and touched the knee of my trousers where they were wet. And then Ronnie suddenly smiled and I knew that I almost had her.

"I always get you in the end," I said.

I knew that I had my hand on the magic string. I didn't have it for long though because Geoff decided to come back at that moment and I shut up shop sharpish. I started to pick over the fruit again. I winked at Ronnie every few seconds, and moved my shoulders up and down in a real comical way because Geoff was behind me, but Ronnie didn't seem to see the funny side of it. She stopped smiling. I think it was because old Geoff had come back and she didn't want to lose her crummy job.

"Is he still here?" said Geoff, loud enough for the whole wide world to hear, if you don't mind.

"Yes," said Ronnie.

"Is he behaving himself?"

It sure made me want to chuckle when old Geoff said "is he behaving himself?" like that, like I was just a naughty schoolboy, or something.

"Yes," said Ronnie. "He's pretty harmless, really. He doesn't frighten you half as much the second time around. You start to feel a little bit sorry for him after a while. I don't think he's right in the head."

Ronnie sure was sweet about the whole thing. You know, telling old Geoff that I didn't frighten her anymore, and everything. Listen, before you try and win over the love of your life, you'd better make sure she isn't frightened of you, okay, because a thing like that sure can ruin a relationship.

Anyway, I sort of turned to old Geoff and fluttered my eyelashes a couple hundred times or more to show him I was "quite harmless", like old Ronnie had said. Old Geoff just sneered though because that is all his type can do in that kind of situation. I think the love we radiated between us - me and Ronnie - just sort of squeezed him out of the picture, if you really want to know, and he sort of felt like he was intruding, which he was.

Anyway, things weren't the same after old Geoff came back and I sort of dissolved into the background where I felt more comfortable. When I left the market I sort of held my hand out and announced to everyone that I was leaving for the day, but nobody seemed to notice.

I always make a big entrance. I come joking and playing up to the party and everybody thinks, *wow, who's this dude?* But by the time I leave they've all more or less forgotten who I am. I can't keep it up, I suppose – you know – all the humorous banter. Well, you just can't, can you? It's a sad thing, of course it is, and I wish it were different, but it isn't. Hey, live with it, okay, because those first few minutes – when you're shining and everything – are like magic. Enjoy those moments because they're gone so quickly and you're going to spend the rest of your life trying to get them back. *Those first few minutes are just the best though, aren't they Jenny?*

5

I didn't go back to my room after that. How could I? Not after the drama of the day. I decided to get a bus from Leicester and go visit Bradgate Park. I sure felt like I was on top of the moon or something. What with old Ronnie almost laughing like that and thinking I was funny, and telling old Geoff that I didn't frighten her anymore. They sure were the good times. I sure as hell figured that if someone tells somebody else you don't frighten them then they must like you a hell of a lot. I really thought old Ronnie liked me a hell of a lot back then.

I sat and stared out of the bus window. The glass was mucky and I couldn't see out much. That crazy bus driver drove like a maniac until I was practically thrown off the seat, for Chrissake. We passed the stone lions and when the water in the fountain brightened the gaps in the dirty window it made me want to cry for some reason. I think I was feeling pretty romantic in general about things. I used to go to Bradgate Park with Jenny. We sure used to have a lot of fun in the old days, when we were just kids and everything.

When we reached Bradgate Park I gave the bus driver a sour look, but he just ignored me. I think he was the kind of bus driver who enjoys it when his passengers are waltzed around in their seats like that. I decided to climb the hill and take a look at Old John. Listen, Old John is a ruined castle that stands on top of a hill or something. Listen, it isn't even a hill, it's a goddamn mountain. When you climb up to Old John you have to avoid the rocks that stick out of the grass and try to cut through the bottom of your shoes. I'd forgotten how steep it was and I had to stop halfway up because I was getting so damn tired all of a sudden. Listen, I'm not a very fit person, okay?

I looked up and saw Old John shining in the wet mist of the sky above me. It was all very artistic and poetic, like in the Scriptures. Listen, there's always a grey, wet mist wrapping itself around Old John, okay? I think it's because Old John almost reaches the sky. Old John is about a million years old and from the top of the mountain you can just about see the whole world. You should see Old John at sunset though, you really should, because it's just about the most beautiful thing in the world. Old John looks at its best at sunset. What I mean is this, if I can try and explain it to you some, if you'll just let me, okay? If you go to Bradgate Park at sunset and stare up at Old John, it will practically burst into flames in front of your eyes. And Old John is so high, they say in Leicester that you can see it from the moon. Well, I was on the moon that day because Ronnie had all but fallen in love with me and I swear I could definitely see Old John.

When I reached the top I suddenly had the urge to roll back down again. That's how I was feeling about things. I wanted to lie on my back and roll down the mountain to find out if you could do it without dying. I also needed to know if it would make you dizzy for the rest of your life. Ronnie sure made me dizzy when I thought about her. I sure as hell loved Ronnie a lot back then, I guess.

I sat down on the grass next to Old John and just stared at the sky. Then I lowered my eyes and looked over Leicester. I was hoping I would see Ronnie, and Jenny. I thought that maybe if I stood up and waved they would see me. Anyway, I did stand up and I did wave. My head was in a bad place back then, I know.

There was another guy there. He was standing close to the edge, peering down the mountain, and I thought he was going to jump off. It looked to me, at least, like he was thinking about suicide. He had a bright red scarf on and, because I was ill, I thought it was the prettiest scarf I had ever seen. The man looked like Michael Caine in *The Muppet Christmas Carol* and I thought it would be a shame if he jumped off because Jenny loves *The Muppet Christmas Carol* more than anything in the world. She loves the song that Belle sings to the young Scrooge, while the old Scrooge - Michael Caine - is hanging about in the background, crying like a mad man, and wishing he'd lived his life differently. Listen, Michael, we all wished we'd lived our lives differently.

Jenny used to sing that song about a million times a day until it just about drove everyone crazy. I sure would love to hear her sing it one more time though. Boy, I think I started loving *The Muppet Christmas Carol* about as much as Jenny did, sitting next to Old John like that. I looked for the man with the red scarf again, but he'd disappeared and I got real scared because I thought he must have jumped. Then I saw the scarf again, blinking, through a patch in the mist, and I breathed a huge sigh of relief. I sure as hell didn't want to tell Jenny that old Scrooge from *The Muppet Christmas Carol* had jumped off the top of Old John, because it would have broken her heart.

I sure felt close to God up there. I don't know. I got to thinking that maybe God lived inside Old John and so I started to stare real hard at the door in case he suddenly came out. And then he did come out, and he came and sat next to me, and it was real spooky, and religious, and pious, and my heart was beating like crazy.

Listen, I wasn't crazy. I knew at the back of my mind that it wasn't God, it was only the man with the red scarf, but I so wanted to be a believer back then, okay? I wanted this guy to take away my sins or something. I don't know. And when God came and sat down next to me, we chewed the fat for a while and I sort of felt glad he was there. Jenny told me that I only thought it was God because of the bang on the head, and I suppose she was right. Listen, Jenny is usually right about these things, okay?

Anyway, old God asked me if I was feeling alright, and I said I was and thanked him for asking. I think he knew all about the bang on the head, what with him being God and everything. He asked me if I realised I had been talking out loud to myself about *The Muppet Christmas Carol*. It was all a little embarrassing, even for me. I told him I did that sometimes. I said I was glad he'd pointed it out though and I sure as hell would try not to do it again in the near future. Obviously I didn't use the word hell in his Holy Presence; give me some credit. I asked him if I could stay and talk to him, so that I didn't look strange if anybody else came along. He smiled and said he didn't mind at all. I suppose that's his job when you come to think about it.

He was listening to his flock. I sure was glad he was there though because there were a few things I wanted to ask him.

"What's your name?" God asked me.

"Franklin," I said.

You couldn't lie to old God like you could to Ronnie. I figured old God knew my name anyway and was just testing me.

"Do you live around here?" he said.

"I was born in Birstall, but I'm living in the city at the moment. I've left home, you see, God. I live near the Angel Gateway."

He didn't seem to mind me calling him God like that and saying it quickly to catch him all off-guard, and everything. I thought it was a good idea to mention the bit about living near Angel Gateway too. He smiled and nodded his head in that godly way of his and I figured he was pretty damned pleased that I had chosen to live there.

"Do you miss your parents?" he said.

Boy, that sure took me by surprise.

"Yeah sure, everyone misses their parents when they leave home, don't they?"

"Have you spoken to them since you left?"

Boy, old God was sure interested in my parents all of a sudden.

"No, sir, no, siree. I haven't seen them much, make no mistake. I saw my dad though. I think I blinked too much. I sure am a disappointment to him. Say, do you know why that is?"

I think old God was impressed when I addressed him as sir like that, all of a sudden and out of the blue.

God sure didn't look how I imagined he would. If you ever meet God – and I hope you do – you take a long good look at his face. I hate to say this about the Creator of the Universe, and everything, but he sure looked like the most insignificant person I ever met.

He sure was friendly though.

"I think you should ring your parents, Franklin, tell them how you're getting on."

There he was going on about my parents again. I was starting to feel a little uncomfortable in his Holy Presence.

"I will, I sure will, and thanks for pointing it out to me. I'm going to go and see them, and tell them how I'm feeling. I'm going to let them know how I keep sinking to the bottom of the sea and how I can't swim back to the surface, and everything."

Old God just nodded in that solemn way of his. He smiled again and I thought, *Boy, old God sure does smile a lot.* He really did though. He must have smiled about a million times on top of that mountain.

"Have you been to the hospital?" he said.

Boy, old God really got to the point. Hell, if it had been anybody else and not God sitting with me up there, I would have told him where to get off. Old God was starting to make me feel uncomfortable, if you really want to know.

"No, sir, I haven't."

"I can take you there, if you like?"

Boy, that really threw me all over the place. Boy, I think I really loved old God at that moment. I was touched that he could find time in his busy schedule to take me to hospital like that. I'll tell you something, shall I? Don't you ever tell me any crap about God not caring and all because I'll spit in your eye and tell you that he does.

"Thanks for that," I said.

I think I must have started to goddamn cry, or something, because old God suddenly leaned over and hugged me.

"I had a son who had some troubles like you," he said.

Boy, I think old God was crying too, remembering about his own son, and everything.

"I know," I said.

I did as well. I'd read the Bible like everybody else, for Chrissake (no offence, sir).

"I wasn't there for him," said God. "I didn't know how he was feeling until a long time after. Until after he was dead."

My goodness, old God was really bucketing tears down his face and everything by then.

"You did all you could, I'm sure," I said.

To be honest, that wasn't strictly true; the bit about him doing all he could. I thought that maybe he shouldn't have let his son suffer and everything like that - you know - for so long. I know he was dying to save our sins and all - but hell - it was his only son when all is said and done.

"I didn't, Franklin, I really didn't. I knew something was wrong, but I just ignored it. I turned a blind eye. I thought he would be alright. A parent just doesn't want to think that their son is different, do they? I knew deep down that he wasn't happy, but I didn't ask him and he never told me. That's why it's so important that you go and talk to your parents, Franklin. It's not too late, for you."

Blimey, I sure felt embarrassed and humble, and everything, sitting there with old God pouring out his troubles to me.

"I'm sure you did all you could, sir," I said. "Listen, I really must be going. I'm meeting my sister."

Listen, I know it was crazy lying to old God like that, when he probably knew I wasn't really meeting Jenny, but I had to get away. He sure was good about the whole thing, he never mentioned it and started making out like he believed me, until I was just about crazy red with embarrassment.

"That's great, Franklin. I'm glad you're meeting your sister. I really think you should talk to her about how you're feeling. Franklin, listen, it's none of my business, but go back home, for God's sake."

Boy, I was confused. About him saying it was none of his damn business and that, when it clearly was because he was The Almighty. And then, him taking his own name in vain like that.

"I sure will, sir," I promised.

I got away from him as quickly as I could. I had to, I swear it. I couldn't take much more. I was sorry I hadn't got to ask him all the questions I'd wanted, but I was feeling suffocated by it all. I started to scramble back down the rocks. I suppose I was crying by then. God suddenly yelled down at me, and I stopped and turned around. He was sitting on a rock. He said the strangest thing to me. He said that I reminded him of his son and it withered me away. I thanked him about a trillion times and then started to climb down the hill again. I was almost slipping down trying to get away from him. Everything was blurry because of the tears in my eyes. I was ruined because

God had told me I reminded him of his son. I stopped at the foot of the hill. I swivelled on the wet grass.

There was a kid running towards me and she was holding a balloon. The balloon was too red for the dismal afternoon and it hurt my eyes. The kid suddenly tripped. She let go of the balloon and I watched it float up towards the sky. I started to run after the balloon. I tried like hell to catch it because the kid was crying and she reminded me of Jenny. I jumped up and down like a crazy man, but I couldn't reach it. I was sorry I couldn't reach it for the kid. I was sick to my heart over it, if you really want to know. We watched it soar away over Leicester and because there was something tragically beautiful about the whole thing, the kid stopped crying. I think we had a moment together over it or something.

When the balloon was just a dot in the sky I looked back at God. Boy, was I staggered. He was still sitting on the grass and Old John looming out of the mist behind him. And believe this if you can: he was watching the balloon float up to heaven and not doing a thing to help. He was even smiling, for Chrissake. Listen, he was perhaps the only one who could get that damn balloon back and yet he never lifted a finger to help that poor kid. I couldn't get over it. I really found it difficult to take in, if you really want to know. Don't get me wrong, I love God - of course I do - but he sure makes it hard for you to like him sometimes. I ran to where you catch the bus and when I looked back for the last time, old God was waving his scarf at me.

6

I used to sit next to the window in my room, staring out, across the market. I didn't even put the gas fire on sometimes because I thought it was romantic to feel cold. Some days there were goddamn icicles dripping off my nose. It's funny, but I can laugh about it now. I'd been back to the market about a trillion times, of course I had, but Ronnie never seemed too pleased to see me. Whenever I tried to speak to her she used to turn her pretty head away. It appeared she didn't love me after all and the truth was shocking. I think she was crazy worried about losing her job. It was all very tragic, and everything. I was walking along the tight-rope of love, I know.

Anyway, I figured that if Ronnie wouldn't speak to me at the stall I would wait for her after work. So I hung around the edges of the market one frosty evening until she'd finished. Christmas was coming and there was a huge tree covered with lights next to the Clock Tower. It was all very meaningful, when you think about it. I'd made up my mind to ask Ronnie if she wanted me to walk her home. Christ, I knew that if I didn't at least try I'd end up wishing I was dead.

So I fooled around for an hour or two – it was five hours – under a streetlamp opposite the market. I was having fun, charging around like a horse and stamping my feet to keep the cold from my toes. It started to get dark and the city lights reflected like crinkled foil on the pavement. There was frost on the ground as well. I swear there was. God, I wanted to cry more than anything if they'd only just let me, okay?

Anyway, after Ronnie finished work she walked towards the bus stop opposite the market and I sort of waltzed up to her. I think I traversed up to her, if you really want to know. I could tell by the look of her face that she was real surprised to see me. She sure looked pretty though. Her face was white and pinched with cold, and I thought I was going to be sick. There was anguish near my heart and all that kind of thing. It looked for a second or two like Ronnie was going to scream and so I told her, quickly, that I'd been waiting for five hours. Ronnie said I looked like I was dying and I said that was funny really because that was how I felt.

Then I handed her a big line.

"Can I walk you home, little girl?"

"No," she said. "Go away."

Ronnie lowered her head and marched away, brushing past me into the bargain, if you don't mind. She left me standing on the pavement feeling like a right lemon. Anyway, I ran after her, I really did. I sort of trailed at her side while she was walking; that fast kind of walk that is almost a run. I was dead cute, I admit it. My hands were clasped behind my back, and I was bowing and stooping like I was her goddamn butler or something. Christ, I sure was laying it on the line for her. Ronnie was worth it though.

"I went to Old John a while back," I said.

It was an ice-breaker, that's all.

"I don't care. Leave me alone."

"I met God. He looked a hell of a lot like Michael Caine. We chewed the fat for a while and then I got away from him. I ran down that slippery mountain they call home. I saw a girl with a red balloon. She reminded me a lot of Jenny. Listen, Ronnie, you're not going to believe this, I swear, but old God never even broke a sweat when that kid's balloon floated off in the sky. Boy, you sure shouldn't have to see a thing like that, you know. It made me feel pretty depressed afterwards, I can tell you."

I was gasping like a marathon runner or something. Old Ronnie was walking so damn fast, she was almost sprinting, and I was struggling to keep up and talk to her at the same time.

"I've got to get my bus. I'm late as it is. That market's so fucking busy."

I sure didn't like to hear old Ronnie swearing like that. Listen, I knew I wanted to marry Ronnie – and pretty soon – and so I knew I would have to tell her that I didn't like women swearing. Jenny swore once and Dad just about hit the roof. She just giggled afterwards though, like it was all very amusing, and everything. She used the F word, for Chrissake. Jenny didn't even know what the word meant, for crying out loud; she'd just heard some kids at school shouting it. That's the problem. You can protect your kid all you want – you know, making it magical – but as soon as you let them out the door someone is going to teach them the F word.

I swear I wanted Jenny to stay at home for the rest of her life, just the two of us. But it can't be like that, can it? And I understand that now, of course I do. You can't lock kids up for ever so that no one will ever teach them a swear word. And you can't follow them down the streets for about a million miles trying to keep your hands over their goddamn ears so they don't hear terrible things. Believe me, I've tried.

"Hey listen, Ronnie, don't swear, okay?" I said.

"You make anybody swear. I haven't met anyone like you."

"Is that good?" I said.

"No, it's not good, it's really not good."

"It sounds good. It sounds like I'm sort of different, you know."

"It's not good. Please leave me alone."

It was time to play the big hand. I knew that. I should have warned her, I suppose, laying down a gorgeous line like this on her so suddenly. But I kind of figured she needed to hear it. I wouldn't say something like this lightly, okay?

"Can you see the stars?" I said. "They're real pretty though, aren't they? They're a hell of a lot like you. Why does everyone have to rush around so much they got to miss the stars, eh?"

Ronnie stopped walking, suddenly, and for a second I couldn't tell if she was going to smile or scream. Then she screamed. Christ, it was sure embarrassing, and all, because when Ronnie started screaming the people walking past stared at her.

"People are looking at you, Ronnie," I said. "You're making a fool of yourself."

"I don't care."

Then I laughed in her face.

If somebody screams at me in the street like that, so that it embarrasses me and everything, then I have to laugh in their face, okay? I can't help it. If I don't laugh, then I'm going to cry.

"Please just leave me alone," Ronnie said, when she'd calmed down a little. "I know you're not well and you're probably a sweet bloke, I don't know, but please, listen to me, I can't help you. I really can't help you. I forgive you because I can see you've got some kind of problem, something sad in you, but why don't you go home to your family? They can look after you. I'm not equipped to deal with this. I've had a really bad day, okay?"

It just about knocked me down when Ronnie said I was "probably a sweet bloke" and everything, and also the part about her forgiving me. Boy, I sure needed to hear it too. I'd been feeling lousy myself; cooped up in my room in the freezing cold. I was at a low-ebb, I admit it. It's funny, and I don't know why I did it, but I sort of leant forwards and said, "Thanks for forgiving me, Jenny." Just like that. I sort of whispered it really, but Ronnie heard me anyway.

"What?"

"Sorry."

"Who's Jenny? What are you talking about?"

"I'm Jesus," I said.

It didn't do any good.

I'd played the big hand and lost.

Ronnie used the F word for a second time that day and then hopped onto her bus, and I never saw her again. Of course, I did see her again, but it sounds more romantic my telling you that I never saw her again, like that.

I love having my heart broken, don't you? Love's like that.

That's what love's all about, isn't it? It's about having your heart smashed into a thousand pieces. That's always the best part, I think. It is for me anyway. It's always best to fall pretty hard when you fall in love. And listen, I always fall pretty hard, okay? I want my goddamn heart broken, for crying out loud. I want to wallow in the pain and self-pity that only love can bring. You know that special kind of pain? Only love can do it right. As soon as everything starts to go well I lose interest. It's not the same anymore. It can't be, can it? I want the crushing pain of love all the time. I want to miss someone so badly it's killing me. And I can't be happy unless I feel like that. Nothing else will do. That's how it was with Ronnie. That's how it is with every girl. They always break your goddamn heart in the end. I swear my heart's been broken about a million times already.

So I stood and watched Ronnie's bus clear off into the night. The lights in the city were fuzzy bright. I was feeling pretty cold, except for my face, of course, which was dripping with sweat. The streetlamps glowed prettily along the pavement and it was perfect as hell. I decided I didn't want to go and sit in my room all night, so went to buy Jenny a Christmas present. I'd decided long ago to buy her a snow globe. Old Jenny loves snow globes just about more than anything else in the world.

There was a brass band playing carols near the Clock Tower and it sounded like the right sort of music to accompany a broken heart. I stopped and listened for a while. I was shaking mostly and crying too by then, if you don't mind. Anyway, a woman from the Salvation Army came up to me and rattled her tin. I pulled out about a thousand notes and stuffed them in her hand. It was too much, I know, and it was still only the beginning of November, but I was confused about things. I swear the sound of a brass band playing Christmas carols can do that to a person. The woman with the tin told me that Jesus loves me and I thought, *If only she knew*.

In the end I just bolted. I had to get away. It was because the sadness was coming back. I could already feel it and I knew I had to get away before everything was ruined. Sadness can do that. It can just about ruin your whole life if you let it.

So I went into that large department store that Mum loves, to buy Jenny the snow globe. I was sweating like a pig. I went to the Christmas section. I found there were about a million snow globes for sale and I sort of froze for a few moments. Then I did a silly thing. I ran along the shelves shaking the snow globes, until eventually things got so sparkly-bright in there I just about went blind. I was going crazy. I was rushing up and down the aisle like a mad thing. I tried to keep all the snow globes going at the same time, but as soon as I shook one, another would stop. It was like trying to balance goddamn plates on sticks, for Chrissake. Pretty soon it wore me out and I sat down in the middle of the aisle and just watched it all for a few minutes. It felt like I was sitting at the bottom of the ocean and the sand had turned bright silver and was swirling around my head.

It's funny, but I was happy while the specks of glitter were floating around inside the globes and miserable when they stopped. Snow globes can do that to you. I wanted to keep shaking them so that I could be happy all the time. I struggled to get back on my feet. My coat was heavy; it felt like it was pressing down on me. Pushing my shoulders down like big hands. God, I really was losing my mind back then. I knew that

I didn't want to buy a snow globe for Jenny after all. I figured that if the bright bits didn't float around for ever then she would never be happy.

I staggered out of the shop because the heat was suffocating me. I could still see the bits of glitter going round and round when I closed my eyes. I raced past the brass band and sat down on a bench near the Clock Tower. I was feeling pretty shaky because I hadn't eaten a thing all day; my head was numb. I stared at the stars over Leicester and they were going crazy too, like the glitter inside the snow globes. I put my head in my hands. I stayed like that for about a hundred years, I think. I was very frightened. Every time I lifted my head to look the stars would sweep past my eyes. I began praying, I suppose. My goddamn knees were shaking like death. I eventually cried out for the stars to stop moving and when I took another look, I saw that they had stopped moving and everything was fine like before. I got calm pretty quickly after that.

I thought about my dad again, I swear I did. It was because of the snow globes. It was because of that day – *that Christmas Eve* – when I ran into the house and told him that Jenny had been knocked down by a car. Dad was merrily wrapping Jenny a snow globe when I told him. The colour just ran out of his face. He gave out a little choking cry when I told him and then he ran out of the house. He never even put his shoes on, for Chrissake.

I remember shaking after he'd gone because I knew he was just about going to die when he saw Jenny lying in the road like that. I just sat down on the floor and finished wrapping the snow globe. I didn't know what else to do. I crack myself up sometimes. I'm the kind of person who will finish wrapping up a snow globe when someone has just been hit by a car or something.

I ran back outside. I was still holding the snow globe. I had wrapped it pretty badly, I admit it. I wanted to give it to Jenny because I knew she'd love it. I wanted to take it right up to her sweet little face and shake it. I couldn't though. Old Dad had her tightly in his arms and was swearing at everybody, even the ambulance men, who came near. When the police came they held my dad down long enough for the ambulance men to wrestle Jenny away from him. Then they put her in the ambulance.

I sort of knew that Dad thought it was my fault. It was too. He'd sent Jenny to look for me because I was late coming home. I was playing football in the road with some of the other kids from the street. I saw Jenny come out of the house and run down the street. She was running towards me, but she didn't see me. She thought I was on the other side of the road. I wasn't even on the other side of the road. *For Chrissake, Jenny, look where you're going.* I just stood there and watched her run into the road at exactly the same time as a car drove by. It was a lousy red Ford Escort. It was the first car I'd seen all afternoon. Back then that road was the safest place in the world to play, I swear it. And old Jenny picked that time to run into the road and look for me. If I had come home on time it never would have happened. Really, it wouldn't have.

As the ambulance drove away I gave Dad the snow globe. Christ, I can't wrap up a present to save my life, I swear it. The paper was hanging off all over the place. He looked at it for about a thousand years and then threw it in the road, and it smashed into about a million pieces.

It's funny really, but Dad always loved Jenny more than he did me. It's not funny. He never said it. I just sort of felt it, I suppose. Mind you, old Jenny was so beautiful you just had to love her more. I swear I would love Jenny more if I had two kids and she was one of them. Of course you would. It stands to reason. You just had to love old Jenny more than anyone else in the whole goddamn world or something. You had to rush out and buy her a snow globe as soon as you saw her, for Chrissake. Jenny was like that. You had to buy a snow globe and shake it next to her face because only then could it be nearly as beautiful as she was. Those magical bits of snow glittering all over the goddamn place were the only things that came near to the beauty of Jenny.

Old Mum tried, bless her. One night, when Jenny was still in the hospital, I came down in the night because I couldn't sleep or something. Anyway, Mum and Dad were sitting on the sofa and they didn't know I was there, and everything. I was really quiet, I admit it. I was like Kwai Chang Caine treading on the rice paper. Anyway, I knew they were talking about Jenny, because I heard Mum say, "It wasn't his fault." I don't know. I knew she meant me. I sort of knew then that old Dad blamed me, and everything, and I think I sat down on the stairs and cried for the first time. I think I hated myself along with him.

You have to hand it to old Mother dear for trying so hard to make him love me. But you can't, can you? You can't make someone love his goddamn kid just by pushing him forwards. You can't just place your kid in front of somebody so they'll notice him and expect everything to be alright. Christ, she just about shoved me across the carpet after him. Mums are like that, I swear they are. They love you so hard they nearly break you and then they shove you up to Dad, to try and make him love you too. It was real hard for Dad though, what with old Jenny running between us all the time, trying to get onto his knee and succeeding about ninety-nine times out of a hundred.

Christ! I sure as hell was depressing everyone, sitting beneath the tower like that. I can be right miserable sometimes. I'll really drag you down with me if you let me. All that stuff about snow globes and Jenny getting run over. Christ! Who wants to hear all that stuff anyway?

I went back to my room in the Angel Gateway. I sat on my bed and stared out the small window until it was morning. I sure as hell was pretty serious back then, I suppose. I sure as hell didn't like being cooped up all alone with myself like that. I sure as hell was getting on my own goddamn nerves. I didn't want to be so serious about life all the time. I sure as hell was sorry that I was the reason old Jenny got run over like that. I sure as hell apologise too much for everything. I sure as hell wish it was me who had been run over and not Jenny that day.

7

Listen, I admit that the next day I wasn't feeling too good. I was shivering all over the place; I'd had a very bad night. So let's be honest, I wasn't at my best to be sure. The damn fine twinkle in my eye had gone. But then I saw the robin and I was happy. I'm just telling you that so you know there was a good reason for me doing the thing I did that day. You know, when I did the thing that I wouldn't normally have done. It was the robin, okay? I admit it. I should have tried to get to sleep, I really should have, but I didn't. It was because there was a robin on my window ledge. It's all about the robin, okay? That robin gave me the best and worst day of my life.

This is what happened that day. *That terrible and wonderful day.* Like I said before, I was feeling kind of lousy. I felt like I wanted to die, if you really want to know. But then I looked out the window and I swear to God there was a robin sitting on my ledge. God! It took me about a million years to get over it. I felt so damn wonderful all of a sudden. He was just staring through the glass like he knew me or something. It's crazy, I know, and you had to be there to understand it, but I sort of struck up a conversation with the little feller. I asked him his name and he said it was Robin, and I didn't know if it really was Robin, or whether he was just pulling my leg on purpose. I just nodded and treated him to a knowing glance, you know, to let him know that I knew what he was doing. He sure was a chirpy little feller though.

Anyway, he told me he thought that I was like a robin and it knocked me out, what with him being my favourite common garden bird and all. He said that I must make sure that I carried on trying to win Ronnie's heart. He said that, at the moment, Ronnie probably thought I was just a sparrow, or something ordinary, but that if I kept going, you know, laying down the magic and everything, then one day soon she would see my red breast. I admit I kind of sniggered when he said breast like that, but he told me to get a grip, for crying out loud. Anyway, he said that if I kept it all going then old Ronnie would see that I was different from the rest.

Mr Robin went on to say that when people first saw me they thought I was just regular, but when they looked for a bit longer they saw my bright red breast. Boy, I was sweating like a bastard when he told me all this. Chirping it all through my window, with the bells of Leicester Church ringing so loudly and clearly in the background somewhere that I could hardly hear him.

Well, then, I did a real crazy thing I'm not proud of. I threw open the window and poor Mr Robin was forced to fly down to the pavement. I looked down and shouted to him.

"Clever robin! Remarkable robin! Go and buy the biggest turkey in the shop window and take it straight round to Bob Cratchit's house."

It was all crazy, I know, but I felt marvellous just the same. I began pacing around my room like a maniac. I was rubbing my hands together. I was deep in thought. I decided that from that day on I would try to be a better man and start looking out for Tiny Tim. I wanted Tiny Tim's welfare to be my concern. I felt a rush of magic sweep through me like fizzy drink at the thought of it all. It was magical. I'd never felt anything like it. My heart was pounding like a bird in a box and I began shouting at my reflection in the mirror. I shouted so damn loud the man in the next room started hammering on the wall. I felt giddy and feverish. I swear I was a little light-headed with excitement.

What I did next was I put on my best white shirt. I was really out of my head with happiness I can tell you. I charged around my room like a maniac. I whistled a merry tune to myself in the mirror and combed my golden hair.

Well, as soon as I was ready I raced down the stairs and out of the door. I ran through the Angel Gateway to the market. I wanted to see Ronnie pretty badly and tell her about the robin. I saw her from a distance, serving fruit, and the sight hurt my eyes. She looked so damn beautiful. Her skin was so white. She looked like goddamn porcelain or something. She was divine. There was a glow around her, I'm convinced of it. God, she really looked beautiful that day. Just about the most beautiful thing I'd ever seen in my whole sorry life. I know I was staring at her through my craziness and you have to take that into consideration when you're summing up, I know, but boy, did Ronnie ever look more beautiful than she did on that day.

I just sat down on the pavement, opposite the market, and cried for about a million years. I think I shouted up at the sky a few times as well. I told old God that I'd forgiven him about the balloon incident and everything. And I knew he had heard me. I knew because it suddenly started to snow. Just like that, while I was sitting on the pavement staring at Ronnie. I couldn't believe it at first; the robin, then the snow. I thought that old God was working in my corner for sure that day.

I moved under a streetlamp to cry a little bit more and then I stopped. I began to imagine that I was inside a snow globe. I was sure that old Ronnie could see me from her stall too. The wind blew crazily all of a sudden, making the snow practically swirl around my head. And I thought that from where old Ronnie was standing it must look like I was standing inside a snow globe. I was a little drunk with the whole idea of love and snow globes back then, I admit it.

I stayed there under that streetlamp pretty much all day, until old Ronnie had finished work. And then when she headed home, I followed her. I stayed behind her so she couldn't see me. I had my hands shoved deep inside my pockets like a hard-boiled detective or something. I followed her and after she crossed the road I crossed it too. Then I shouted her name and she stopped.

She turned around. I was a little disappointed because when Ronnie saw me she sort of froze with horror. It really looked to me, at that moment anyway, that I was perhaps the last person in the world she wanted to see. My heart sank a little, you know, because of the look on her face and everything. Anyway, I carried on regardless. She kept on walking, with her head down, and I had to take my hands out of my pockets to keep up with her. When I finally caught up with her I sort of lingered by her side for a few hours, you know, grinning like a kid, and everything, trying to break the ice between us, I suppose.

Suddenly she stopped and glared at me.

"What do you want?" she said. "It's getting late."

Boy, I sure was upset, what with her looking at me as if I was poison or something.

"Can I take you away from all the madness?" I said.

I took hold of her hand and then swung it around a little, real playful, like we were kids in the playground or something.

"No. We've been over this all before. What is wrong with you? Can't you just leave me alone?"

Ronnie pulled her hand away from me like it was stuck in a bear trap or something. Boy, she sure was sore at me for some reason.

"I've been here all day," I said.

I was grinning like a cat. I started nudging her with my shoulder and rolling my eyes something terrible until it hurt.

"I don't care how long you've been here, please leave me alone."

"But the snow," I said.

"What about it?"

"I was dancing in the snow. I was doing it all for you. And then God, in his ultimate wisdom, decided to shake everything up for us. He did it in front of your eyes. It was like a snow globe or something."

"What are you on about?"

"Jenny loves snow globes."

"Why do you keep talking about this Jenny?"

"Why, are you jealous?"

I sniggered again and put my hand across my mouth.

"No, I'm not."

"Jenny's my sister," I said.

"Why don't you go and speak to her?"

"I wish I could."

Ronnie was standing so straight she was like a sentry outside Buckingham Palace or something. Her face was white, and tense, and pinched. She looked scared, or concerned, about something.

"Chill out," I said, and nudged her some more. "Relax a little, why don't you?"

I started waving my hands around. It was some kind of mystic martial arts, that's all. I was trying to make her feel less tense. She just glared at me.

"You look so sad," I said. "Do you know you look like a young Carson McCullers?"

I was pulling out the big guns, and I knew it.

"I don't even know who that is."

Ronnie looked at her watch. Then she put her head to one side and I nearly passed out because her hair flopped down onto her shoulder. She had a puzzled look on her face that was adorable.

"You know. *The Heart is a Lonely Hunter?*"

Then Ronnie got up really near to my face. So close, in fact, it scared me a little. She started whispering things, terrible things, and her breath was like white smoke in my eyes.

"Listen, you fucking little creep, if you don't stop pestering me I'm going to get Geoff to kick your face in. If I ever see you again I swear I'm going to scream and tell people you're a rapist, okay? Now fuck off and don't ever bother me again. You're a mental case. Please go and crawl under a stone, you repulsive, weird little maggot. You disgust me. Don't you know that? Every time I see your slimy face it makes me cringe. It's getting to the point where you're starting to frighten me again, okay? Now fuck off and don't ever talk to me again. You're a freak and a loser and I can't help you, okay? Now please go away and die."

Ronnie said the terrible things with her beautiful mouth and all the time the snow was melting on her tongue.

Then Ronnie turned and walked away from me. She went into the Angel Gateway and I watched her go. I stayed there for about a hundred years after, or something, talking gibberish to myself, you know, trying to think about what Ronnie had said, trying to digest it all. I was crying and laughing, I admit it. I admit everything. The words die and rapist were going round and round in my head. I kept walking away and returning to the spot where Ronnie had said all those awful things. I was agitated. I started biting my hands real hard.

Then I heard Ronnie scream.

I kid you not. Ronnie screamed from inside the Angel Gateway. Then I heard a rough-sounding voice telling her to "shut the fuck up". He also said it would be "a lot less painful" for her if she let them get on with it.

The voice terrified me; I wanted to put a hundred miles between me and the Angel Gateway. I loved Ronnie, sure I did, and everybody knew I did, but I still thought about getting away from there just about as fast as I could. I visualised getting back into bed and pulling the covers over my head. I could see pictures of myself doing it, but when I came to the part where I put the blankets over my head I heard Ronnie scream again.

And I didn't run away, ladies and gentlemen. *God bless me, everyone.* I knew I would have done, before the old bang on the head, but on that day I did not. Well. This is what I did next. I put my hands in my pockets, real casual-like, and began sauntering towards the alleyway. I must have looked real tough to the on-lookers, I admit, and also, because I started swaggering a little too, they probably mistook me for a New York gangster. Anyway, keeping up all the swaying business, I went into the dark opening of the Angel Gateway.

Well, as soon as I got in there, I heard Ronnie crying from somewhere in the shadows. It halted me in my tracks for a second. I also realised how dirty it was in there all of a sudden. The walls were covered with graffiti and swear words, and I decided on the spot that I sure wasn't ever going to take Jenny in there.

The light began to improve the longer I was in there, as it always does, and when I saw them holding Ronnie down all my courage slipped down onto the wet filthy floor. They had her dress up and I could see her legs, glaring white, and it made me want to be sick. I leant against the wall for a little while to compose myself. There was a leaking pipe, sticking out of the wall, and the bricks below it looked a beautiful red colour. I stood up straight and took some really deep breaths. God, I remember wishing I was my dad. I felt dizzy, and hot, and cold, and scared. I admit I wasn't your typical hero.

Then Ronnie screamed real high, suddenly, and my heart shattered into a thousand pieces. I slapped my face hard to work up some colour. My cheeks were stinging, but it worked and, somehow, I felt better. After another huge breath I continued with the swaggering and sauntering towards Ronnie and the naughty men.

There were two of them, skulking in the shadows. One was black and one was white. I was shaking badly, my breathing was noisy, and the white guy turned and looked at me. It stopped me in my tracks. I took my hands out of my pockets and stared back at him. I smiled and then gave him a friendly wave. He just kept staring back at me for about a million years. It looked like he couldn't believe I was there. I couldn't believe I was there. He had a real nasty glint in his eyes. He was unshaven. Then the other naughty man, the black one, turned and looked at me too. They both just stood there watching me for a long time after. Ronnie was looking at me too and because her dress was thrown nearly all the way over her head, I could just about see all her underwear and things. Things that I knew I wasn't supposed to be seeing.

"Fuck off," said the white man.

He spat it out like phlegm or something. He didn't look too happy over the fact that I was there.

I looked down at Ronnie. She sure looked scared to death. Like a small frightened child. She wasn't my Ronnie at all. I really needed to tell her to pull down her dress because it was just about killing me.

"Yeah, fuck off, mate," said the black man, who was bigger than the white man but not as cruel-looking. In fact, his eyes were quite sad, like mine, and I kind of felt sorry for him for a while. I don't know what I felt. I sort of felt everything and nothing at all. I was more terrified than I'd ever been in my life. It was also the calmest I'd ever felt too. My heart was racing, but my mind was clear. I felt as if I was going to sleep. I felt the coldness in the air, but my limbs were warm.

"How you going there, fellers?" I drawled. I tried to sound as friendly as I could. I wanted to get things between us off on an even footing.

"God! Please help me," Ronnie moaned from the ground.

It tore me in two the way she was looking at me. I smiled at her. I nodded too, so she knew that everything was going to be alright. Ronnie started to cry. When Ronnie cried it looked like her whole face was falling to pieces.

"Shut the fuck up, bitch," said the white man, and pulled Ronnie's dress up some more. Ronnie's thighs sure were white, even in the dark shadows of the Angel Gateway, and I kind of looked at them for a moment. They shone like candles. They were sexy and terrifying.

"Yeah, we're going to get to you in a minute," said the black man, grinning some.

"Easy there, fellers," I said.

"Fuck off, mate, else you're going to get badly hurt," said the white man.

"I can't," I answered him real politely.

"Just walk away now."

"Come on, chaps, I can't do that, can I?"

"You really need to walk away now, mate, or things are going to get bad for you."

"Things are already bad for me," I said.

"Just go."

"Why would you want to do a thing like this? Ronnie's a real sweet girl, she really is. Okay, she can get nasty sometimes; you know, calling me a freak and everything, but I don't think she meant to say it. She really didn't mean it. I'm sure she didn't. I don't think she meant it, you know, fellers. I'm really hoping that she didn't mean it, okay? She wouldn't tell people I'm a lousy rapist, not really. You're the real rapists. I'm not a rapist. Please don't tell Jenny I'm a rapist, okay? Jenny thinks I'm just about the greatest person in the world. Do we have to tell Jenny I'm a rapist? It would sure break her heart and all."

"Are you a nutcase?" said the white man, and the black man giggled behind him.

"I'm afraid I might be. I'm real terrified that I might be."

"You're going to die today, mate, if you don't go away."

"Does it really have to be today? Come on, fellers, it's snowing outside, for Chrissake. A man shouldn't have to do his dying when it's snowing. That sounded like John Wayne. I'm not John Wayne. I wish my dad was here."

Then the white guy went and pulled a goddamn knife out from somewhere. He stepped towards me and started waving it around next to my handsome face.

"If you don't fuck off quick, I am going to do you some serious harm."

He sure was waving his knife around like he was real proud of it or something.

"You sound quite educated."

"Fuck off."

"*Language, Timothy!*"

I sort of joked with him, trying to fool around a little until the cops got there and saved the day. Christ, I couldn't even hear the sirens.

And then he did a really strange thing.

He moved forwards some more, real causally, like he wanted

to hug me or something, and stabbed me. He really did it. I was totally shocked when he did it, I can tell you. I just looked into his eyes and shook my head like I was real disappointed in him for doing it. And do you know what? I never felt a thing. I just sort of glanced downwards and watched him push the knife into my chest. He did it real slowly, carefully, almost artistically, if you must know. He did it all quite beautifully. I can remember thinking how clean and shiny the blade was before it went in my chest and how red and bloody it was when it came out again. It didn't look at all clean and shiny when he pulled it out and I don't think the nasty man thought so either because he looked at it with disgust and then wiped it on the wall next to him.

"Fucking hell," said his mate, you know, the sad-looking one. "You've killed him."

Then the white man, who had stabbed me, did a funny thing – to my eyes anyway. He sort of did a silly little Irish jig and then motored away. I think he was real sorry for what he had done. His mate spat at me and ran off too. Ronnie was still on the floor and in shock too, I shouldn't wonder.

But Ronnie, bless her, didn't shout or anything; she just got up and pulled her dress down, which I was real glad about, I can tell you. Then she came towards me. Some of her dress was still riding up and when I pointed to it she had the decency to straighten it out. God, Ronnie sure looked full of concern for me all of a sudden. She looked at me in a real tender way and it sure was a relief at last. It was real good to see her looking at me like that, especially after all the nasty stuff.

I was starting to feel real dizzy. I was beginning to feel the pain for the first time. I sort of staggered back, against the wall, and Ronnie gasped and it echoed around the Angel Gateway. Ronnie put her hand over her mouth. Then I thought that she was flying above me, like an angel, but she wasn't, it was because I'd slipped down the wall and was lying on my back. The ground felt wet.

I was gone, man, I can tell you. I sure felt cold and hot, and everything. I could see old Ronnie, looking down at me, but she was spinning now and I couldn't focus on her. I wished she would stay still. The walls in the Angel Gateway were jumping up and down. Then Ronnie's face dissolved, or something. I began to panic then, you know, when Ronnie's face went blurry like that. I closed and opened my eyes a few hundred times, but she was still fuzzy, and I heard a gasping sound that came from my own throat. A great pain erupted in my chest, suddenly, and I think I cried a little. Actually, I think I cried a hell of a lot. I sure hated the fact that old Ronnie had to see me crying like that.

When I looked down at my chest I got a big surprise. The blood was beginning to spread over my clean white shirt and I started to imagine I was a robin. And as the darkness in the Angel Gateway crept closer, tugging at me, I remember thinking that looking like a robin was a nice thing.

8

But Tiny Tim did not die.

It sure still depresses me though, when I think back on it all. Even now, when I'm lying in the darkness, it sometimes comes sweeping back and I have to bite my hands to make it stop. Anyway, the consultant said I was lucky to be alive, which was funny really, because I didn't feel lucky.

I must have stayed in the good old Leicester Infirmary for about a hundred years. It sort of struck me as kind of funny, seeing as that was where I was born. The nurses didn't seem to remember me though. They sure were pretty - and yes - I suppose I started flirting with them a little to pass the time of day. I think I must have broken about a thousand hearts while I was in there, for Chrissake. Anyway, I was still alive; apparently the knife had missed all the vital organs.

Jenny was sitting by my bedside one day when I woke up. There was snow floating past the windows and she never even had a coat that I could see.

"What are you doing here?" I said.

"Charming, I'm sure."

"I know you don't like the sight of blood, so don't look at the plaster."

"Typical. Still he thinks everything's about him. Why's it always got to be about you all the time?"

I smiled. Jenny sure looked cut up though, seeing me like that.

"Where's your coat?"

"I don't need a coat. You're a revelation. You don't get it at all, do you?"

Jenny started to chuckle for about a million years. It got on my nerves a little, to tell you the truth. Jenny always has to chuckle for about a million years. It sure was good to see her happy though.

She stopped suddenly.

"You were very brave," she said. "Who would have thought it? My brother the hero? God, I'll probably just about never hear the end of it."

Jenny folded her thin arms and sat back heavily in the chair.

"What's wrong with you?" I said.

"I don't know. Things have changed. What with you being a hero now."

"Are you proud of me?" I said.

"Of course not. God. You're going to be impossible."

"Not even a little bit?"

"Maybe a little bit."

We both smiled.

A nurse suddenly came up to the bed. She didn't seem to mind that Jenny was there.

"I'll have to get an extra chair," she said. "Your parents are here to see you."

Boy, it sure shook me up when Mum and Dad arrived

unannounced like that. Jenny gave me a frightened wave then ran away and hid. The old folks stood staring down at me from the side of the bed. It looked like they didn't recognise me at all. Mum's mouth was an O shape, for Chrissake. Mum said, a long time afterwards, that what shocked her most was the little plaster stuck on my chest to cover up the knife wound.

I was embarrassed they had to see me like that. I kind of hated myself for letting them down. They sure had high hopes for me, I guess. I wished I'd made it to Leicester University like they hoped I would. I sure began to wish I'd made something of myself.

Mum started speaking real fast. Her mouth was smiling, but her eyes were full of terror, or something. She talked about everything except the stabbing. Poor Dad just stared at me like I was the saddest thing he'd ever seen in his life. Then Mum suddenly stopped talking and started to cry, and it just about broke my heart to see it.

When Dad spoke I think it was the first time I listened.

"You look terrible, son."

"Gee, thanks, Dad."

"What's happened to you?"

He didn't mean the stabbing either.

Mum stopped crying, but there was an awful lot of sniffing going on.

"I feel right lonely sometimes, you know, missing you both and everything," I said.

I was really pouring it out for the old folks, no messing, trying to make everyone in the whole world feel sorry for me again. I do that a lot. I love it when the whole world is taking pity on me. I love putting on a real brave face and pretending I don't want to talk about it when I'm practically dying for you to drag it all out. I felt like I was taking away all their sins, or something. I'm just about the most charitable person in the whole world sometimes.

"Why don't you come back home, son?"

Mum laid a tender hand on my head and then sort of mussed up my hair like when I was a kid.

"I'd love that. I really would and I will soon, of course I will. I sure miss you both to hell, I really do. I'm burning to crawl back home and beg for your forgiveness."

"Why are you talking that way, son?" Dad spoke quietly. It was like he was afraid of me all of a sudden.

He glanced nervously at the other beds in the hospital. I took a peep at Jenny. She was back at the end of my bed, nervously chewing the blanket around my feet. She was cuter than mom's apple pie. She looked anxious though, so I winked at her to make her feel better. She was mouthing something at me, but I couldn't tell what it was. I think it had something to do with Dad. I think she was telling me not to get him all fired up.

I nodded at Jenny and then turned to Dad.

"Sorry, Dad, I sure am sorry about that. You know, about talking so goddamn fast all the time, practically shouting it out, so the whole world is staring at us and embarrassing you half to death in the public bar, and everything. You know, ripping up all the beer mats and not drinking the landlord's fine ale."

"Stop it, son."

"I will soon, I sure will, Dad, of course I will. Hey listen,

I'm sure looking forward to coming home for Christmas, okay? Spending Christmas together again like we all used to. A real traditional affair with mince pies and all. You sure make the best damn mince pies in the world, Dad. And old Jenny will be so pleased when I come back and she'll probably want to kiss me about a million times and hug me half to death in the hall, I shouldn't wonder. And then we'll open all the presents under the tree. I love a real tree though, don't you? I love the smell of the pine needles."

"Stop it."

"I can't stop, Dad. I'm afraid I can't stop it. I want to stop, of course I do, but I can't. I'm real scared now, Dad. I want it to stop now please."

"Please, don't, son."

"I'm practically bursting out of my head waiting for Christmas day. I sure as hell want old Jenny to see the snow globe I bought her. Boy, but doesn't Jenny love snow globes more than everything? And it's just about the best snow globe you ever saw in your life. Old Jenny's going to just about love it more than all her other presents put together."

"Jenny's dead," said Dad.

"I know."

"Oh son," said Mum.

"I never even bought her a snow globe," I said.

Dad couldn't take it anymore. Couldn't stand it, I suppose. All that talk about Jenny and snow globes. He broke down in front of us and who could blame him? Certainly not me. I swear it was the only time I ever saw him cry. He never cried, even when Jenny died.

He rubbed his eyes with the back of his tattooed hands and fought to get himself under control. I wasn't helping, I admit it. I was grinning like the Cheshire Cat for some strange reason. Listen, if something real important like that is happening I have to laugh at it, okay? A great sob seemed to pass through Dad's giant body. It was sure sad having to see him like that.

I looked at Jenny. She was biting her lip something rotten. She shook her head and mouthed that I'd done it now for sure. Then Dad suddenly stood up and rushed out of the ward, and I stared at Mum, real shyly, like I'd never met her before. I was drained seeing my dad cry like that.

"I've been talking to Jenny a lot lately," I said.

I glanced down at Jenny for support, but she had gone.

"What?" said Mum.

"I've been seeing Jenny. She comes to my flat sometimes and starts chatting to me. I don't know how she gets in because I always lock the door. Sometimes when I wake up she's just sitting on the end of my bed, staring at me. It sure is good to see her though."

"You're not well, Franklin. You need to come home so we can look after you."

"I know it's not right, seeing Jenny, I mean, but I'm happy to go along with it. I love it when she visits me, if you really want to know. It's just about the best feeling in the whole wide world when she comes to see me. We just have a little chat. It's all pretty cosy and innocent. We chat about the old times. It's the only time I'm happy."

"You frighten me when you talk like this, Franklin," said Mum.

"It's only because of the bang on my head. That's what Jenny said anyway. And you know how damn clever Jenny is. She said I'll only see her while I'm ill. She says that when I'm better I won't see her anymore. Mum, I don't want to get better if it means I can't see Jenny again. She sure misses you and Dad a lot. She told me about a hundred times that she sure would love to come back for Christmas just one more time."

"Oh God." Mum put her hand over her mouth.

"I'm going crazy, Mum."

I said it jokingly, but it still scared me half to hell hearing myself say it like that. I thought that maybe if we both laughed we could somehow keep it all at bay. I knew that if it took me over completely, I was finished.

Mum got up and kissed me on the head. Then she stroked my hair some more. It felt damp, she said. She also told me that I was dreadfully thin in the face and my eyes looked kind of wild. I think Mum used the word feral. She took about a million pounds out of her purse for me and then made me promise to come home when I got out the hospital. She told me Dad wanted me to come home too, but was finding it hard to tell me because he was so strong, and everything. I said that I sure would try and make the effort and that I practically couldn't wait until we were all safely back together again. I meant it as well.

9

They gave me some tablets in the hospital that tasted foul and I couldn't swallow them too well, but they sure made everything seem a whole lot better. I still take those pills when I get down about things. They make me see things differently. The consultant at the hospital told me to go and see my GP (General Practitioner), for Chrissake. He said I needed to get some proper long-term medication and psychiatric help. He said he thought I was probably manic depressive, or something, for crying out loud. They sure as hell were more concerned about my goddamn state of mind than my wound. I stayed at the hospital for a few weeks. When they eventually let me out it was nearly December. On my last day, I went and sat in the gardens to look at the wire statues they've got there. It was a dismally grey day and I was the happier for it. Listen, you'd better understand that I'm not too good with sunshine. Sunshine can always depress you, okay?

Then, while I was sitting there, taking in the world, I saw Ronnie. She was standing staring at me through the glass in the cafeteria next to the gardens. I watched her fold and unfold her arms about a million times or more. She looked shaky, and sad, and pretty, all at the same time. It also looked like she was shy about coming outside and talking to me. Well, I made it real easy for her. I beckoned her to come hither and she sort of shuffled through the door and towards me. Her head was bowed and her arms were folded tightly. She had a drab grey coat and untidy hair, if you want all the crappy details.

"Hello," she said.

Ronnie's voice was so quiet it nearly tore the hospital walls down. Her face was white, but not a healthy white like before, rather a sickly white that made you feel a little ill yourself to look at it. It looked as if her skin was tinged with blue, like when you put a spot of ink in milk.

"Sit down, little girl," I said. "Before you blow away you look so thin."

Ronnie sat down heavily, so close to me, in fact, that my love for her came back in one wonderful, sweeping rush. I couldn't speak for once, I really couldn't. I just sat there gazing at her.

"I'm so sorry," she said.

"Why?" I said, knowing full well why.

"Talking to you like that. *Saying all those awful things.*"

"Don't get upset," I said.

I was trying to make it easy for her, I admit it.

"I'm so very sorry. I can't tell you how sorry I am."

Ronnie sounded real lost and it choked me up.

"Anything for you," I said.

I couldn't think of anything else.

"Why would you do that?"

"Why wouldn't I?"

Ronnie was shivering badly and getting worked up, I

shouldn't wonder. Her breast was heaving under her coat. It was moving so damn hard her arms were moving up and down with it. God, I felt so uncomfortable all of a sudden. I knew that I would probably laugh pretty soon, if she didn't get herself under control pretty quick. I can't deal with people's breasts heaving around like that. My head was aching badly and the pain in my chest wasn't from the knife wound. It was all very romantic.

I stood up suddenly. I had to break the tension. I was unravelling again. I cracked my fingers and then pulled on my imaginary braces, stretching them as far as they would go without snapping. I held my head solemnly and wagged a finger at her. I think I tried to look stern. I walked to another bench, a few feet away, and sat down. I wouldn't look at her. I stared at the grey sky. I took a deep breath in, sighed, and shook my head wearily. It was all very dramatic and done for effect. I thought I was in a goddamn movie or something.

I decided I'd let her suffer enough. Listen, if you drag that sort of thing out too much you're going to ruin it. I didn't drag it out too much. I let it carry on just long enough. I was crazy with excitement when Ronnie came and sat down next to me. The excitement was rushing through my veins like electricity or something. It sure was nice having her follow me around like that. It felt good knowing that old Ronnie would probably follow me to the end of the world if I asked her to. It would have been a pretty cruel trick though, when you think about it.

"I understand if you never want to see me again," she said. "But I needed to come and see you to say thank you."

"Thank me?" I whispered it. I looked at something behind her head – a blackbird in a tree, I think – and tried to focus on it.

"Thank you," she said.

"You don't need to thank me, Ronnie."

"Yes, I do. I can't get any of it out of my mind. What you did for me. The way you stood there when he put the knife into you. I've watched it over and over again in my mind. *The look on your face when he did it.* I can't get your face out of my head. You just watched him do it and then you smiled back at him. You had the calmest face I've ever seen. You didn't even seem to feel the pain for a long time. I can't get over it. I'm a total wreck. I can't sleep over this. Please forgive me. All those terrible things I said to you and then you did that. I feel ashamed. I'm so sorry."

"All in a day's work for Superman." I stood up and whooshed my coat around like a cape. Then I sat down again.

"And all the time, all the fucking time, all you do is joke. I can't get over it as easily as you can. It's driving me crazy. The way you are. I can't stand it and I don't know why. I can't stop thinking about it. I can't move on with my life until I know why you did it."

Ronnie looked terribly sad and all I could do to help was crinkle my nose. I began to cough. I clapped my hands because they were frozen with the cold. I felt weak suddenly. I was floating in the sky and looking down at us both, sitting on the bench. I was having an out-of-body experience, I'm certain of it. I didn't feel in control of my faculties. It was because I'd lost all that blood, I suppose.

"Please answer me. Why would you do that?"

"I did it because I love you," I said.

"That's bullshit. That's from story books and films, for crying out loud, that's not real life. No one does that in real life.

Please! I almost wished to God that you hadn't done it. Don't you understand that? I can't deal with it."

Old Ronnie sure was getting worked up. It was beginning to get a bit embarrassing. I'm like that. You can be pouring your heart out to me and telling me the most important thing in your life, like you love me, and everything, but if you're raising your voice then I'm going to feel embarrassed. Ronnie was shouting louder than I used to, for Chrissake. It was a proper reversal of fortune kind of thing.

"Just say you'll walk out with me, little girl, and we'll say no more about it."

"What? I can't believe any of this."

"Believe it, angel face. Just go walking out with me one night. Any night, tonight for Chrissake. Just a heartbreak stroll around the Clock Tower and back."

"I don't understand you."

"What's to understand?" I said, rather coyly, if you don't mind. "I love you."

"My head's all over the place," she said.

"So is mine." I grinned.

I still kept a sense of humour about it all.

"I don't know what to do."

"Just go out with me, one time, and then if you don't absolutely have the best night of your life I'll never bother you again."

I drawled it out all in front of her. I fluttered my eyelashes to get the full effect. I was hoping I didn't faint before I heard her answer. My lips were turning blue, I shouldn't wonder.

"Okay. I suppose I owe you that."

10

I was over the moon when old Ronnie agreed to go out with me like that. I felt tired after she'd gone, and dizzy, and when my chest started bleeding again I had to holler for the nurse. I was terribly weak and light-headed a lot back then. I had to lie back down on the pillow for a moment because black patches were gobbling up my eyesight.

When they let me out later that day, I went back to my room in the Angel Gateway. I think I slept for about a million years. When I woke up old Jenny was sitting on the end of the bed, staring at me. She had the saddest expression on her face. I told her about Ronnie agreeing to go out with me, but she just sulked and pulled a face.

"That's nice for you," she said in a way that let you know she wasn't overjoyed about the whole thing.

"What's the matter, old Jenny, my sweet? It doesn't mean anything, really, you should know that. You're the only girl in the world really for old Franklin. Jenny, please don't look so sad. Jenny, you're frightening me now."

"It's alright for you."

"I thought you'd be happy for me."

"I am," she said, and then started crying all over the

place until it just about broke your heart in pieces.

I wanted to put my arm around her, but I knew it wouldn't do any good.

"I'm sure sorry you're dead, and everything," I said.

Jenny started sniffing until it all but got on my nerves. I pulled a few goofy faces and Jenny looked at me with those big brown eyes that can just about kill you if you're not careful. Then she smiled.

"That's better," I said.

Boy, when old Jenny smiles at you like that it just about lights up the whole world. It's like a million stars exploding in the night sky or something.

"I'm pleased for you really," she said, through damp sniffles.

"I sure wish I were dead instead of you."

"Don't you dare say that," she said.

"Why, it's true, isn't it? I meant to ask God about it."

"I told you already. That was because of the bang on your head."

"I know, already. I'm not crazy, you know?"

"Listen to me before I get cross, okay? It wasn't your fault that I got run over that day, okay? I should have damn well looked where I was going."

"Let's not talk about that," I said.

"We've got to talk about it, Franklin. You've got to start taking responsibility for your own life. Stop hiding in the shadows. Face up to the real world. You live in a fantasy world, for Chrissake."

Old Jenny started laying down the law, and everything, like only she could. She sure seemed to be in a foul mood for some reason. I didn't know where to put my face or anything. Jenny can sure get worked up when she's in a mood. I'm glad you weren't there. I sure as hell wouldn't have wanted you to have seen all that. I sure was spineless in the face of it too. And even now I'm kind of embarrassed when I think about the whole thing.

When old Jenny had finished, she came and hugged me, and said that we wouldn't mention it again. She said it was all water under the bridge. Jenny also said that if I didn't simply have the best night of my life with Ronnie she'd probably never speak to me again.

I met Ronnie near the Clock Tower. I didn't think she'd show up, but she did. She looked beautiful and I knew I'd go anywhere with her. We sat holding hands for hours. We never held hands, okay? We were both a little shy about things, I suppose. I was proud that she was next to me.

"Look," she said. "There's a party going on at my friend's house."

"Friend or fiend?" I said. Ronnie ignored me and moved a lovely bang of hair from out of her eyes.

"Would you like to come? You could meet some of my friends."

Ronnie seemed to hold her breath tightly after she said it, almost as if she hoped I would say no. Hey, listen, I know that I said I would go anywhere with Ronnie, but I sure didn't want to go and meet her lousy friends. I was so damn insecure and everything by then I wanted to kill myself. I hate all those social bashes, don't you? I just wanted the girl all to myself. I was so terrified that Ronnie would meet someone who would make her laugh more than I did. You can understand that, can't you? If it isn't all about me, it just isn't worth it. Look, I'll love you to death, but if you start laughing at something someone else has said I'm going to leave you, okay? I won't stand for that. It doesn't matter if you laugh at something that one of your girlfriends has said, but if you laugh at another boy, well, I'm going to hate you for the rest of your life. It's all very immature and insecure, I know.

"We don't have to go if you don't want to," Ronnie said.

"No, hey listen, I'd love to go, of course I would."

I really didn't want to go by then. I wanted to cry. I felt so damned depressed all of a sudden. I wanted to go home because everything was ruined. It suddenly felt like all the happiness had been sucked away and the walls were crumbling down next to me. One minute I'm wildly happy, the next the whole wide world is falling down around my ears. Boy, it sure is exhausting living your life like that. It's like all the happiness rushes away because it can't stand to be around you.

I knew that me and old Ronnie were doomed from the start. I knew that it would all end in tears like everything else. I knew it would all come to nothing and I was happy about it in a strange, bizarre kind of way. Listen, you'd better understand that I love all that heartbreak stuff that comes afterwards, okay? I fall in love about a million times a day, okay? You'd better believe it if you're intending to stay with me. Listen, you'd better break my heart quickly before I break yours. And listen to this next bit. When I fall, I fall pretty heavily. I mean, I fall from the greatest height you can possibly imagine and I smash into about a million tiny pieces. I know this is all sounding a little crazy, and everything, but I just wanted you to know that, you know, before you decide to start falling in love with me and everything. I'm going to try and break your goddamn heart before you break mine. It's the only decent way.

Don't you just love all that kind of thing though? Isn't it what the world is all about? Really, what else is it about, if it isn't love? We all want to fall in love, don't we? And we all want to be loved? Yeah, that's right, I reckon. It's funny; I seem to know so damn much about it, you'd think I'd get it right. I seem to hold on to it too tightly, I suppose. Like Ronnie's hand. I'm not happy unless I'm crushing the life out of it. I'm not totally happy until I've completely destroyed everything.

I'm happier when I'm wandering around, half dazed, in the battlefields afterwards. If I'm happy for too long, I start thinking that something isn't right. I start to look around for things to go wrong and as soon as you do that things do start going wrong. It's like I think I don't deserve to be happy. I'm good with misery, but I'm not too comfortable with happiness. I don't trust happiness like I do misery. Listen, you know where you are with misery and you know that nobody else is going to want to get a part of it. But happiness? Well, I just don't know. I reckon the whole world will want to try and take away your happiness.

Listen, it's exhausting trying to hold on to your happiness. It's much easier to let it go. It's easier living with misery because you can turn your back on it. And you know that whatever happens, nobody is going to creep up and steal it away. Yeah, that's right, I suppose. I think that's how it is.

Anyway, that's how we ended up going to Ronnie's friend's

party. Listen, you'd better understand that I hated Ronnie's friend right from the start, even before I met him. As soon as she told me his name was Danny I hated him, okay? If Ronnie had told me *her* name was Debra then I would have liked *her* for sure, but when she told me *his* name was Danny, I just knew it wasn't going to work out too well.

When I saw the swell, semi-detached house, I was a little nervous about walking through the door. I'm not too comfortable around large numbers of people. If I see a crowd I sort of go to pieces. I start saying crazy things just to try and impress everyone. Listen, it doesn't impress anyone, so don't do it. Anyway, as soon as I collapsed through the door I started coming out with all the crazy stuff that was supposed to be funny. You know the kind of stuff I mean, okay? Anyway, it was so damn loud in old Danny's house nobody could hear me anyway and I spent the whole night practically screaming the place down. Isn't life a bit like that though? You spend your whole time screaming the place down and nobody is listening.

Anyway, I sort of lost Ronnie in the general hubub of things and found myself a shivering and a dithering, and alone, in the kitchen. My fingers were hovering over the delectable nibbles, but I kind of knew all along that I wouldn't be able to eat any of it. You can put a mountain of food in front of me at a party and I'm not going to eat it, okay? Listen, if some stranger who I've never met before hands me a plate of food that they've prepared with their own hands then I'm just not going to eat it. Not in a million years. Listen, if you ever invite me to your party – and I hope you never do because I won't come – you'd better just hand me a goddamn unopened packet of crisps or something. Look, if you offer me a nice tuna sandwich that you've just made then I'll run a mile. Listen, if you make me a cheese and pickle sandwich at least I'm going to think about it, okay?

I eat so damn slowly as well. And it's pure torture if you've got to watch something like that. Listen, when I was a kid I choked on a sandwich and since then I have to chew my food for about a thousand years before I can swallow it. It's all in the mastication for me, I suppose. Boy, it's exhausting when you have to chew your food for a million years or more because you think it's going to choke you. You really can't enjoy food when you eat that way. It's also agonising for other people to watch, okay, because they don't know why the hell you're eating so slowly. In the end they just watch you because it's all so strange and compelling, and everything, and they can't help themselves. Hey, I'm not blaming them, okay? Listen, it's far better if I eat by myself most of the time.

Anyway, I needed to go outside pretty soon, I figured. I'd lost Ronnie for sure, I knew that. Christ, everybody knew it. Old Danny boy knew it for sure. The music they were playing was so damn loud I couldn't hear myself think. Old Danny boy sure had a lousy taste in music and all. Listen, if you don't play "Little Girl So Fine" by The Asbury Dukes then I'm probably not coming to your party, okay? I wanted to be in the cold outside because I felt cold inside. I wanted to be by myself because I knew that was how it was always going to end. I grabbed a can of pop and went outside.

Anyway, I sort of lingered outside the back window for a while, looking in at the fun. I wasn't part of the scene back then,

I suppose. I moved away from the house when I couldn't stand it anymore and strolled around the garden for a few hours, you know, walking up and down the lawn, staring at the flowers in the light from the house. The moon was hanging in the sky above me and everything was pretty for a while.

There was a sweet little pond in the garden, with a plastic bridge over it, and when the moonlight shone on the water it glittered with the reflection of the stars. I was starting to feel romantic again and my heart began to ache for Ronnie. It was aching for anyone by then, I suppose. Jenny came and sat down near the pond and I reminded her about the time she threw my *Yellow Submarine* in our pond back home to see if it would float. Of course, it didn't float; it just sort of sank into the filthy water. It twinkled once or twice before disappearing forever in the murky depths. Listen, that *Yellow Submarine* was about a million years old, okay, and worth a fortune. I was fuming, but old Jenny thought it was all very amusing and just laughed at me. In fact, Jenny started to laugh again, while we were sitting there. The music from the house sounded thin and the moon was leaning forwards in the sky, peering down, and the stars were twinkling.

Anyway, I sat down on a wet stone next to Jenny and listened to the water tripping over the stones. I love all that water lapping across the rocks, don't you? I could practically sit down and listen to the tinkling of pond water all night. And the moon was throwing down silvery lances all around me. I was bursting with romance. I was practically begging to see old Ronnie's face by then and it sure had a lot to do with the moon, I think. Jenny told me to get back in the house immediately and fight for Ronnie's love, and I told her that I jolly well was going to as well.

I looked at the moon one more time. I swear I could see Ronnie's face in it. I really could. Jenny couldn't though and said I was fantasising. She was all smiling and glowing. I sort of blew her a kiss, which is ridiculous, I know, and she winked back at me in a real friendly way. I felt so happy again I was practically bursting. Anyway, when I couldn't stand being away from Ronnie any longer, I sort of dragged my sorry ass up off the stone and went back into the house to find her. I wanted to tell her I was sorry.

Jenny called out, "Way to go, Franklin."

Well, when I got back to the kitchen and saw Ronnie sitting with old Danny I felt sick.

They were a-huddled and a-cuddled together in a corner and she had her arm around his neck. Old Danny was crying about something and so I started crying as well. I wanted to run away and die. It felt like somebody called Ronnie had kicked me in the heart or something. And I think I was crying a hell of a lot louder than old Danny by the time Ronnie turned around. I caught a reflection of myself in the kitchen window and I looked real upset, I admit it. The look on my face chilled me to the bone, if you really want to know.

Ronnie smiled weakly at me, but then turned back to old Danny boy again. She didn't even notice I was crying, for Chrissake. I hated old perfect Danny boy by then for sure. Listen, I think I've always hated old Danny, okay? I felt so damn insecure about everything. I swear old Danny boy was trying to cry louder than I was and I felt pleased about it for some reason.

In fact, I dragged a chair from the kitchen table and sat myself down to watch him for a while. He sure was turning on the waterworks for old Ronnie's benefit.

"Come on, don't cry," said Ronnie, so tenderly it just about killed me to hear it.

Hell, Ronnie, I was crying too, you know.

Then Ronnie stroked Danny's wonderful blond hair in a way that made me want to cut it all off his goddamn head. I'm so jealous and insecure all the time, I swear it. I felt she must love him for sure. Elvis Presley was singing "The Wonder of You" somewhere behind me. I wanted to tear Ronnie away from old crying Danny and dance a little with her. Listen, I'm the best goddamn dancer you're ever going to meet. Listen, when I dance, people watch. That's how good I am.

"They're playing our song," I said.

"What?"

Ronnie turned on me sharply. It cheered me to see the hate back in her eyes.

"It's Elvis, babe."

I shrugged my shoulders like there was no need for any explanations. I think I even curled my lip for her like Elvis would have done.

"Can't you see that Danny's upset?" she said.

"Yeah, I can see that. Of course I can see that."

Well, old Danny boy started to cry even louder when old Ronnie mentioned the fact that he was upset, and everything. It was all done for effect though. He was making a right old song and dance about it, and it made me feel sick to have to watch him. I was the only one who could see right through him though. I swear when Ronnie wasn't looking he had a goddamn grin all over his face. He was getting a real kick out of Ronnie stroking his hair as well. I think I shook my fist at him and said "Why I oughta."

"Can you leave us alone for a minute?" said Ronnie.

"You came here with me, Ronnie," I said, in a sad, serious way that I was kind of proud of afterwards.

"I know, but Danny's upset," said Ronnie.

Well, old Danny boy hollered even louder.

"I know he is, of course he is, but we don't like Danny, do we?"

"I like Danny," she said, and old Danny grinned all over his face again.

"I know you like Danny, but you don't love him like you love me, do you?"

I'm telling you straight – when I reminded Ronnie that she loved me old Danny boy just about sobbed the place down.

"Danny's dad died a few months back," said Ronnie, sharply again, like I should have known all about it or something.

"I'm sorry about that, of course I am," I said.

"You should be."

Ronnie said it in a real hostile way too. I looked at old Danny boy. He'd stopped crying and was waiting for me to react. And when Ronnie started stroking his face I knew then that everything was lost. I knew it was over for us. I think I'd known it all along. We might have made it too, Ronnie and me, if it hadn't been for old Danny's dad dying on us like that.

I don't know why, but I just started laughing at them both.

I couldn't help myself. I couldn't stop even if I'd wanted to and I did want to, believe me. I was like the goddamn Joker or something.

Ronnie looked horrified and old Danny boy started getting worked up again. He sure wasn't helping much.

I just kept on laughing. I really did, although inside I was feeling frightened. I think I knew then that pretty soon I was going to start screaming.

Ronnie was still glaring at me. I put my hand out to her, for help, but she just held old Danny boy even tighter. He was practically wailing by now. I kept on laughing, but my reflection in the kitchen window behind them looked terrified. *Real terrified.*

So, of course, I started screaming. There wasn't anything else left to do. I was laughing and screaming for a few seconds and then I was just screaming. Of course, everybody at the party came into the kitchen to watch me scream. They looked at me real closely for a few minutes, like they couldn't believe it, and then they got hold of me and bundled me into the street. And Ronnie didn't even try to stop them. She just watched me with an awful look on her face. I wasn't a big hit with her friends, I admit it.

I think that by the time I was thrown outside I was screaming pretty intensely. I was pretty scared too because I didn't know where I was. I didn't know the way back to the Angel Gateway. It was the end of the road for me, and I knew it. Christ, the whole world knew it. Old Danny boy knew it for sure. Like I tried to tell you before: once you start screaming you're finished.

Just a small note here before we go on. When they were turning me out of the house old Jenny turned up and tried to stop them. She was begging them to leave me alone, but they didn't seem to hear her. She said I was her big brother and they hadn't seen me in the best light, and that really I was a pretty decent sort of feller. In the end she just sat down on the front step and sobbed. I just wanted to say that for the record. *Jenny, my precious.*

Anyway, I couldn't stop screaming and that's what terrified me the most. I thought I was going to be screaming for the rest of my life. I figured that as soon as I woke up in the morning I would start screaming. The only time I wasn't going to scream was when I was asleep and if I couldn't get to sleep, I would just lie in my bed screaming. That was how it was going to be from now on. I was convinced of it.

Anyway, I ran up and down that old street screaming until the police came and threw my sorry ass in a van.

11

So they put me back in the hospital for a while. The Psychiatric Ward, for crying out loud. They crammed a whole lot of pills down my throat and, gradually, I stopped screaming. It was pretty hairy for a few weeks, but finally they got everything under control. I don't want to dwell on the dark times too much, okay? The upshot of it was that if I kept taking the pills I would be fine and if I stopped, I wouldn't. They also said that if I took the pills I would be out for Christmas.

Jenny came to visit me, of course. I woke up one time and she was sitting in the chair next to my bed. Her arms were folded pretty tightly and I could see she was real uptight about something. She hadn't even brought me any grapes, for crying out loud, and Jenny knew I loved grapes just about more than anything else in the world. Listen, if you ever visit me in the hospital you'd better bring me grapes, okay, or I won't even speak to you.

Anyway, I started chewing the fat with old Jenny for a while and the people in the beds next to me didn't seem to mind too much, what with her being dead and not really there and everything.

Anyway, after the pleasantries, old Jenny cut right to the chase.

"This is probably the last time I'm coming, you know?"

After Jenny had said it she sort of looked out the window behind my bed for a second or two so she didn't have to see the look on my face. Listen, old Jenny knew I wouldn't be too overjoyed about the whole thing.

"Yeah, I know, but why?" I said.

"Because you're getting better."

Jenny sure was fidgety. She started looking at her watch like she had somewhere important to go all of a sudden.

"Am I? I don't feel any better," I said.

"Yes, of course you're getting better. It's the drugs they're giving you in here."

It sure amused me when old Jenny said the word drugs like that.

"What drugs?" I said.

"I don't know what they are, do I? I'm not a doctor, you nincompoop."

Old Jenny was always calling someone a nincompoop ever since she'd heard the word on a radio show. It's just about the best thing in the whole wide world though when Jenny calls you a nincompoop.

"You're a nincompoop too," I said, and we both laughed for a while.

"Has Ronnie broken up with you then?"

"Yes," I said.

"Sorry about that. Was it because of the screaming?"

"Yeah, I suppose so. Girls just don't like that kind of thing."

"Don't worry," said Jenny.

"Thanks for trying to stop them throwing me out the house like that."

"That's okay," she said, shrugging her shoulders like it was nothing.

Jenny was being real good about the whole thing, you know, not rubbing salt into the wound, and everything. Jenny's pretty decent about the important things.

"She was pretty though, wasn't she?"

"Just about the prettiest," I said.

"Did you love her?"

"Yeah, I suppose I did. In my own way. Not as much as I love you though, you nincompoop."

We both laughed again.

"She wasn't right for you," said Jenny.

"Yeah, I know."

"You've got to find someone more suitable."

"I always pick the wrong ones, don't I?"

"Yes, I'm afraid so. Who's *Gregory's Girl?*" she said.

"You are," I said.

"Listen, there's something important I want to tell you."

Jenny's voice sounded a whole load more serious all of a sudden and my heart dropped in my chest.

"What is it?" I said.

I was sure breathing pretty hard as well for some reason.

"You've got to go home now. After you're better that is, of course. If you don't then I'm going to smack you."

We both laughed again. Old Jenny was always threatening to smack someone.

"Why do I have to go home?" I said.

"Because Daddy's forgiven you."

"Has he?"

"Oh yes," she said. "Everybody knows it. In his heart he knows it wasn't your fault I got killed."

"I don't like it when you start talking about getting killed like that," I said.

"Oh for Heaven's sake. You've got to start facing up to things, you know. How are you ever going to survive if you don't start facing up to things?"

Boy, it sure tore me in two when old Jenny started talking about facing up to things like that.

Jenny stood up to wipe away a tear that had fallen down my face. She did it with a grubby piece of tissue she pulled from her sleeve. She had to stand on tiptoes to reach me, for crying out loud. Jenny was always pretending to be Mum until it just about drove you crazy. It sure made me feel sick when she spat on the tissue to clean my face. It sure is the greatest feeling in the world when old Jenny is wiping your face with a tissue though.

"Have you spoken to him?" I said, weakly, after she'd plonked herself back down in the chair again.

"Of course not, I'm dead," she said.

Jenny was giggling again, like it was just about the funniest thing she'd ever heard in the whole wide world.

"Why are you laughing?"

"You're the only one who can see me, you nincompoop."

"Is it because of the bang on the head?" I said.

"Yes! Finally, the penny has dropped. Well done. Give him a clap."

"How do you know he's forgiven me then?" I asked.

"I just know, that's all. I know these things."

"Smarty pants," I teased her.

I was starting to feel a little brighter about things in general. Old Jenny was starting to fade before my eyes.

"You're fading away," I said.

Jenny glanced outside the window and sniffed about a million times. I don't think she wanted me to see the tears in her eyes. Old Jenny was always looking out the window when she didn't want you to see the tears in her eyes.

"It's because you're getting better, you silly thing," she sobbed. "Don't you know anything? Blimey, I thought you understood it all, but now I'm not so sure. You're hopeless."

"Don't go," I said.

"I've got to. It's for the best, you know."

"I'll never forget you," I said.

"I know. Blimey, you're far too sentimental for your own good."

"Am I?" I said.

"Yes, but it's why I love you bestest of all."

"Bestest isn't even a proper word," I told her.

"Now who's the smarty pants?"

I stuck my tongue out and Jenny pulled a face.

"Oh, your tongue's horrible and yellow." She screwed up her eyes in disgust.

"I can hardly see you now," I said.

"Good, that's the way it should be. Now, remember, you've got to go home when you're better. Mum will make you a nice bread and butter pudding when you get back. Your favourite. Oh, I hate bread and butter pudding. And I'll only eat the custard if it's not too lumpy."

"You're a funny one," I whispered.

"Make sure you come and visit my grave. And bring bluebells. You know I only like bluebells. Oh I used to love the bluebells in Swithland Wood."

"Stop talking about graves and all that; it's upsetting."

"Oh I could scream. I have to treat you like a child."

"I can hardly hear you anymore. Speak up, child."

"God, now I've got to just about shout it all over the place."

"Don't blaspheme," I said.

"You old silly."

I remember when she was alive, Jenny was always saying how much she hated having to "shout it all over the place" because I never listened to her. I *was* listening, I used to say. Jenny said I never listened because I was always too busy reading some boring old book or something. I told her I could read a boring old book and still listen to her at the same time, for Chrissake.

Jenny was right though; sometimes I didn't listen. Jenny spoke so damn much sometimes you couldn't listen to it all. If Jenny were here now I sure would listen to every word she said.

I had the merest notion that Jenny leant over the bed and kissed me because I felt a damp tingling sensation on my cheek. I thought I saw her smiling too and then, just before she disappeared altogether, she stuck her tongue out. I only saw her one more time after that.

I recovered pretty quickly. The drugs really helped. The doctor said that although I wasn't cured entirely, if I kept taking the pills, things could be controlled. He said I would never have to scream again if I didn't want to; I told him I didn't want to. He said it was high time I started living normally again. He also went on to say that it was time to come back into the light. He said I had to look upon my life as a single day, made up of hours, and that what had happened recently was just one small hour of my life. He told me I had had my hour in the darkness and that it was time to come back into the light. He sure seemed to know what he was talking about as well.

Like Michael Caine said – when he wasn't being Scrooge and everything – if you haven't got peace of mind you haven't got anything.

I left my flat above the Angel Gateway and went back home. Mum was waiting for me on the step. Dad wasn't there. I thought he was probably down the pub, but Jenny said just you wait and see. It was Christmas Eve and Dad had hung up strings of coloured lights around the windows. The sky above the house was bluish and there was a slight fall of snow and it was all as perfect as hell. I hesitated at the gate. I looked down at Jenny. She gave my hand a squeeze. She told me to get straight in the house before she had to get cross. I smiled. We both knew it was the last time I would ever see her and I was glad about it in a morbid kind of way. I put down my bag and knelt next to her.

"I'll never forget you, Jenny," I said.

"I should hope not. Now get up, you're frightening Mummy."

I stood back up and smiled.

"Jenny, I feel scared about the future."

"Franklin, my dear, I don't give a damn," said Jenny.

"Goodbye, funny face," I said.

I opened the gate and walked up the path. Mum was holding out her arms. I saw Dad. He was behind her in the hall.

He was smiling too. They both hugged me for about a hundred years on the step. Then they went in. I looked back. Jenny was waving at the gate; she looked kind of faint and I could see the snow falling through her.